MIDLIFE MOUNTAIN SASQUATCH

RENEE BRUME

Hot Mess Express Publishing

CONTENTS

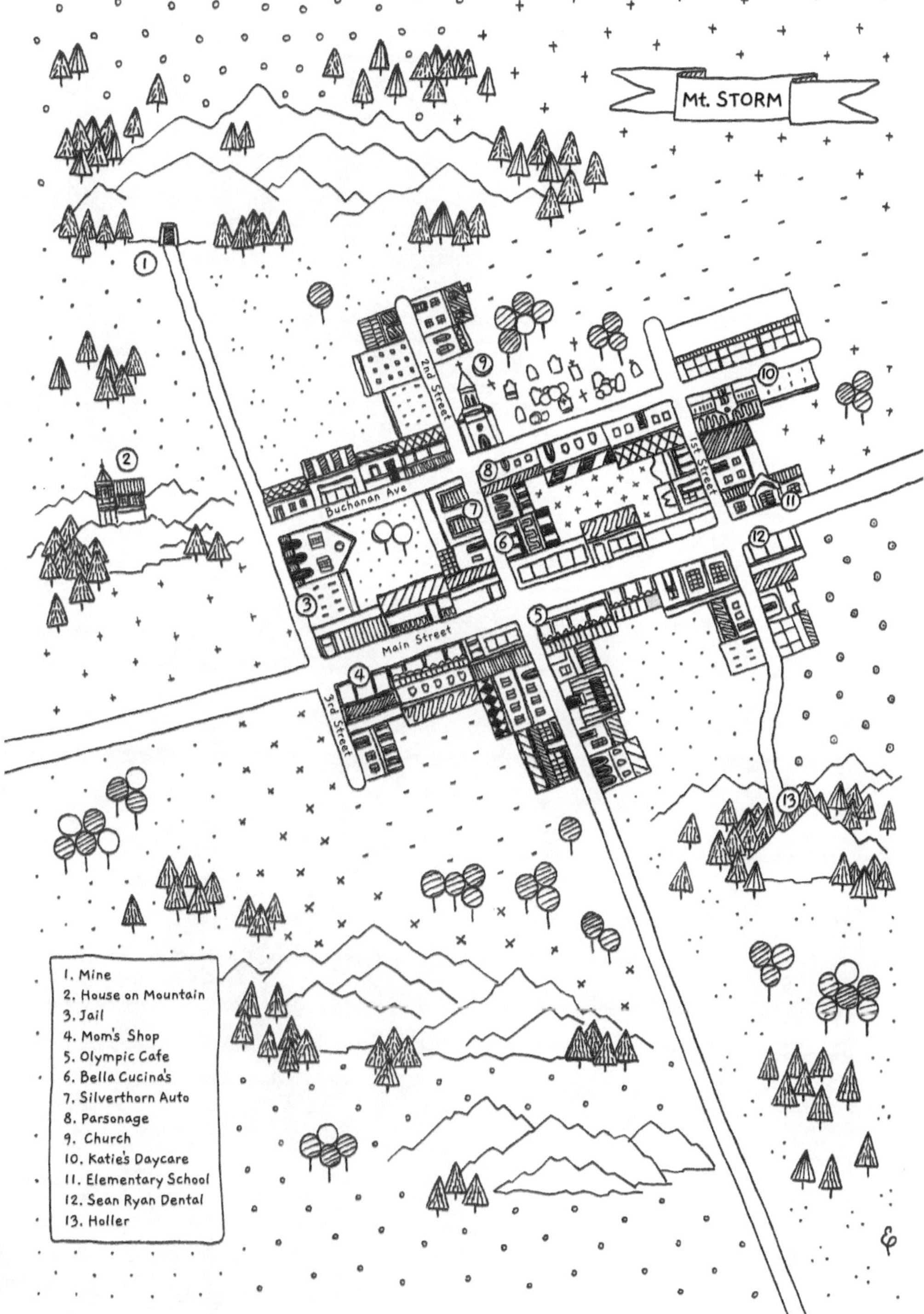

Mt. STORM
2nd Street
1st Street
3rd Street
Buchanan Ave
Main Street
1. Mine
2. House on Mountain
3. Jail
4. Mom's Shop
5. Olympic Cafe
6. Bella Cucina's
7. Silverthorn Auto
8. Parsonage
9. Church
10. Katie's Daycare
11. Elementary School
12. Sean Ryan Dental
13. Holler

PROLOGUE

The dark shapes moved silently through the forest, stalking their prey. A smell, foul and rank, followed, but the wind was blowing the stench in the wrong direction. At nearly ten feet tall, the thickly-haired Sasquatch should have made more noise, but a lifetime in these woods had taught them how to hide until they wanted to be seen.

His feet, bare and thickly calloused, felt the leaves on the path, and he let out an audible grunt as he began clamoring down the slope, his dinner-platter-sized hands covered in fur, grabbing at the trees for support. His brothers followed, their brown and rust colored fur hiding them in the shadows of the trees.

They were the Wright Sasquatches, otherwise known to cryptid hunters as Bigfoot. Thought to be part legend and local myth, they were very much real and dangerous. If a Sasquatch didn't want you on their land, they would find a way to make you disappear.

The family had been here for as long as anyone could remember, living in the forest, at home among the cedars, firs, and rich wildlife that populated this part of the world.

Eventually, many of them were hired by the National Park Service. Their innate knowledge of the forests and ridges of the Pacific Northwest made them perfect rangers.

That's what Russ Wright was when he slipped into his weak human form: A park ranger in the Mt. Rainier National Park. He lived with his large extended family nearby. His parents ran the lodge, and he kept the peace and tended to the trees. It was an arrangement that worked for everyone.

Today, he and his brothers were investigating a pack of werewolves that had moved into the area. And they weren't from any local pack they knew. These were strangers who had arrived seemingly from nowhere. The werewolves were disrupting the peace of the National Forest, scaring not only the wildlife but the tourists who had spotted a glimpse of them while out on family hikes and picnics.

Below him, he spied the wolves, their dark backs turned against them, looking down the hill. He stopped, holding up his massive hand. His brothers, Blake and Morris, stopped behind him, their breath huffing through their widened noses.

He crouched down, the rough bark and leaves of the tree breaking up their silhouette. The forest went silent, as it usually was when the Sasquatches walked, and his ears strained to make out noises from below.

But the werewolves just sat and watched, their ears flicking this way and that. Russ's breath slowed, along with his heart rate. He could sit here for hours, not moving, becoming one with the forest.

His brothers were like stones behind him, and he reached out his mind to Morris. *"What do you think they are doing?"* he asked telepathically.

"Waiting for something," Morris replied, his eyes blinking slowly.

Blake didn't reply, his eyes were like gleaming river stones. Finally, life snapped back into his eyes, and he made the connection to them instantly. *"There are more coming up the mountain."*

They settled in to watch and saw another group of wolves approach. Now, there were a half dozen of them. With interest, he noted that one wolf was completely silver. Not from this area at all, in fact…

He shook his head slowly; he had only met one other pack of werewolves that were silver, but those werewolves lived in West Virginia. It seemed inconceivable they were this far away. One thing he knew about werewolves was that they were territorial. He had been asked, though, to keep an eye out for any strange werewolf activity. This was strange, all right.

And then the werewolves shifted, glowing purple, taking their human forms. In their hands were long rifles. He knew those weapons and knew they were filled with deadly silver bullets.

His eyes went wide, and he turned his head slowly to look at his brothers, his heart rate increasing.

He dropped the connection, and let out only one loud grunt, which meant "Run!"

CHAPTER 1
SEATTLE

I looked out the airplane window as we approached the Seattle-Tacoma International Airport. The Space Needle rose out of the steel and glass skyline, and snow-covered mountains loomed in the distance. I could almost smell the cedar and pine in the air flowing from the overhead vent.

The business jet's wheels kissed the ground and then came to a stop.

"Sam," Easton said in his deep, velvet voice, "do you think your brother would kill you if given the chance?" He was a huge wizard, dark-skinned, with eyes behind sunglasses and a wand on a shoulder holster.

"A year ago, I would have said yes," I said, grimacing. "He wanted the leadership of the pack bad. He never thought a female should lead. But he fled here and helped me escape once. It would have been easy enough for him to just kill me. Maybe he's still got a shred of decency left in him."

Garret frowned, his lips blood-red against his pale face. He was a vampire, and he pulled up his ever present hoodie in preparation for us leaving the plane. "Junior's also been hardheaded. I wouldn't put it past him to double-cross you for his own gain."

The flight attendant and pilot stood at the front, saying goodbye as we exited out of the business jet. The Seattle air was cold and damp, and the afternoon sun was weak through the overcast skies. I'm sure my vampire friend appreciated the dim sunlight. Although he had the ability to turn into a raven and fly, he didn't.

The mountains in the distance reminded me of home, but the sea to the east was a wholly different thing entirely. My sharp werewolf nose picked up the scent of salt in the air, mixed with the diesel from the airport.

We headed for the rental counter, and Easton slid his driver's license across to the agent. "We'll head out to Ashford tonight. We should reach the lodge by five."

"I'm a little nervous about this. How are we going to hunt down Orchium and my brother? Do you think they are here in the city?" I said, looking out the window at the skyline.

Easton gave me a little smile. "I'm already on it. Russ Wright reported that Orchium is in the area. He and his brothers have pinpointed the area they are working in."

"And we are staying at the lodge?" I asked, happy to be back in the area. Maggie and I had taken a brief trip here after our wedding a few years before, staying with the Wright Sasquatches at their family lodge. It had been a magical trip, and I was already anxious to run through the wilds.

"Yeah, we are staying at the Wright Lodge, located near Mt. Rainier. Russ and his brothers work for the park service, but his family has run the lodge there for generations."

"I just hope they can give us some insight on the werewolf packs in the area," I said as we went around the corner of the parking garage and found our rental car, a four-wheel drive white Bronco.

"It's not a long drive. We should be there in about two hours," Easton said, sliding behind the wheel. He liked to drive, and since he seemed to know where he was going, I was not opposed.

"I'll follow you from the air so I can get familiar with the area," Garret said, looking up at the sky. He looked right and left to make sure no one could see him and then transformed in a quick flash of purple to a black raven.

I slid into the passenger seat, clicking my seat belt closed. We headed east out of the city toward a range of mountains, a raven chasing us the entire way.

We pulled up at the lodge right around five o'clock. It was a huge log structure, three stories, with a massive entrance hall. It seemed like Mt. Rainier was so close I could reach out and touch it.

The Wright Lodge was nestled in the Nisqually River Valley, just off Highway 706. The town of Ashford had everything visitors to the parks needed. A gas station, a general store, lodging, and several bars. It had a charm all its own.

Surrounded by huge pines, a quick perusal of the map showed the network of trails in the area, as well as an abundance of fishing outfitters and mountain tour groups.

The main entrance to the lodge was busy. An old, grizzled man worked the front counter, his eyes sharp. As we walked in, they brightened. "Easton!" he said warmly. "We've been waiting for you and your group."

"James!" Easton said with a smile, dropping his bag. "This is some place you have here. When you told us you ran a lodge, I was expecting a small collection of cabins. This is like a five-star hotel."

"Pssst," he said with a smile. "We only have about fifty rooms, and we like to think we are more homey than fancy. I did build this all myself, but I had a little help."

"Well, it's good to be here. It was a bit of a long plane flight, and with that drive…" Easton said, leaning on the counter while Garret and I looked around. My vampire friend looked very uncomfortable, but maybe it was the floor-to-ceiling windows that took up the entire front of the building.

"Let me get you keys to your room. You wanted them side by side, right?" he said, pulling out some keys.

"Yes, these are my friends, Sam Silverthorn, head of the Silverthorn werewolf pack, and Garret Valencia, Potentia's vampire expert. We need a top-floor room so he can come and go easily."

Garret fixed his purple eyes on him and touched his lips; they looked dry. "Where you able to secure my special menu?"

His smile fluttered briefly, and he said, "Yes, of course. It was a bit of a challenge, but Blake is a certified paramedic with the ranger service, and he managed to find what you need at the nearest hospital. The blood bags were left in the mini-fridge in Garret's room."

"Thank you. From here on out, I'll be able to hunt for what I need," Garret said, looking slightly embarrassed. "Animals, of course."

"I should hope so," James said in a slightly irritated voice. "The boys are somewhere nearby. They said they would meet you all for dinner at around six. My wife, Pearl, has a private room reserved for you at our restaurant."

"Thanks," Easton said, handing me a key with the number 312 printed on it. "Can't wait to see Russ."

I couldn't believe that old man built this entire place with his bare hands. Some of the logs were massive. And then I remembered he was secretly a Sasquatch and shivered. The strength it would have taken…

We made our way to the stairs, the soft hum of conversation from the lobby fading behind us. The rich scent of polished wood and aged leather filled the air as we ascended the grand wooden staircase, its banister gleaming under the warm, amber lighting. The staircase spiraled up to the third floor, its steps creaking faintly under our feet

I noticed that our rooms were side-by-side as we had requested, with my room in the middle. The hallway was lined with thick, woolen carpets in deep earthy tones, muffling our steps as we walked. The walls were adorned with more black-and-white photographs, each capturing a different majestic angle of Mt. Rainier.

"Meet downstairs at six," Easton said. I nodded, feeling the cool brass of the doorknob as I turned it and stepped into my room.

The room enveloped me in warmth. A large king-sized bed dominated the space, its thick, green and brown plaid quilt inviting and plush. The faint scent of cedar lingered in the air, mingling with the fresh, crisp scent that wafted in from the slightly open French doors on the far wall. The furniture, impossibly heavy-looking, was crafted from thick logs, each piece sturdy and rustic. Yet another black-and-white framed photo of Mt. Rainier hung on the wall above the bed.

But I didn't need the photograph, because this room had a balcony, with a small, round table and two chairs made of wrought iron. Pushing open the French doors, I was greeted by the most breathtaking view of the actual mountain. The snow-capped summit of Mt. Rainier loomed majestically, glowing softly in the late afternoon light. The air was crisp, carrying with it the faint scent of pine and the distant sound of birds calling as they returned to their nests.

I sighed, a deep, contented breath that momentarily eased the tension in my shoulders. Tossing my bag onto the sturdy dresser, the sound of it landing was a dull thud against the solid wood. I clicked on the news, the low murmur of the television blending with the soothing sounds of nature outside. The screen flickered to life, casting a soft glow across the room as I tried to get a feel for the area before dinner.

This trip was business, but it was personal, too. I hoped I would be able to put an end to my family problems once and for all.

The thought lingered as I stood on the balcony, the cool breeze brushing against my skin, and the mountain standing silent and steady in the distance, as if waiting for me.

DINNER WITH BIGFOOT

The dining room was filled with guests at dinner time, and as we approached the hostess stand, a little old lady with a charming smile dressed to the nines greeted us. Her gray hair was piled on her head, and a pair of reading glasses dangled from a silver chain around her neck.

"Our special guests!" she greeted us in a husky voice, brimming with hospitality. She picked up a handful of menus with practiced ease. "I'm Pearl Wright. You met my husband earlier."

"Lovely to meet you, Pearl," Easton said with a genuine smile. "I've had the pleasure of meeting Russ, can't wait to meet the rest of the family."

"Oh yes, Russ is our traveler. He went all the way out to West Virginia to meet your boss a few years ago. He's been itching to talk to you—there have been some developments that have us worried," Pearl said as she led us through the crowded dining room, weaving between tables filled with guests enjoying their meals. The clatter of plates and the hum of conversation faded as we approached a set of closed French doors at the back of the room. Pearl opened the doors with a flourish. "Boys, your friends are here!"

Inside the private dining room, the atmosphere shifted to something more intimate. The walls were paneled in dark wood, and a crackling hearth fire provided a warm, inviting glow. The faint scent of pine lingered in the air, mingling with the mouthwatering aroma of fried chicken. Three large men, clearly brothers, sat at the table, each nursing a pint of beer. They wore worn park ranger uniforms—tan shirts, olive pants, and sturdy work boots. Their iconic tan felt Stetsons were set aside, and three pairs of sharp eyes flicked to me and Easton as we entered.

"Welcome. We've been waiting anxiously for your arrival," Russ said. "Come, sit down and eat with us. My mom's fried chicken is on the menu tonight."

We took the empty seats at the table, and a waitress came to take our drink orders. I really wanted a beer, but recently, I quit drinking. It had become a problem, which was ironic since my family ran a Moonshine Distillery. The problem is, I liked drinking way too much. It helped me stop thinking of the weight of my responsibilities. Now was not the time to start up my bad habit again. I had to find my brother, stop Orchium, and save the world—in that order.

So, with a sigh, I ordered water, and then we all put in our dinner orders. Everyone but Garret ordered the chicken. "No, thank you," he said. "I already ate. I'll just have that glass of red wine, please."

The men all exchanged looks as Russ introduced them to us as his brothers, Morris and Blake. "My cousins are around too. We all live in the area. If you happen across a lone cabin in the woods, it's probably my kin."

I nodded. "I know the feeling. It's good to see you again,

Russ, and meet the family. I wish it could have been under better circumstances."

A concerned look crossed Russ's face. "We got eyes on your brother. He's in the area with Orchium."

I let out a deep sigh. "I can't believe Junior left West Virginia, let alone joined up with a criminal organization. It's inconceivable. My father didn't raise us to be like this. He detested drugs."

"As do I," Morris said, his deep voice booming. I noticed that Morris had a long scar on his hand, disappearing up his rolled-up shirt sleeve.

"Well, we are here to track down Orchium," Easton said. "You've seen them in the area?"

"My brothers and I patrol this area. Officially as rangers and unofficially as protectors. We've gotten reports from tourists that they had seen wolves around the lodge, which is rare but not unheard of. We have two packs just north of Mt. Rainier. But these were far too frequent to be normal, and the sightings occurred in the middle of the day," Russ said, concern on his face as he took a sip of his beer.

The dining room was a cozy yet robust space, with dark wooden beams crisscrossing the ceiling and a roaring fire crackling in the stone fireplace at the far end of the room. The air was thick with the scent of roasted meat and herbs, mingling with the rich, earthy aroma of red wine.

The third brother spoke. Blake was thinner and shorter than his brothers and obviously the youngest. I noticed he had the medical patch on the shoulder of his green ranger shirt. His mouth turned up into a cocky smile. "Naw, I knew the moment I saw them, they were no good. I figured out the general area where they were, and my brothers and I tracked them to the north end of the mountain, near Old Desolate Peak."

"That sounds ominous," Easton said with a grin, his voice carrying just enough to blend with the ambient noise of the room.

"It isn't so bad. I know how to take care of werewolves," Blake said, giving me a wink. The flickering candlelight on the table made his eyes sparkle mischievously.

I chuckled, both at his brash attitude and his shameless flirting. "You ever been in a werewolf fight?" I said, cracking my knuckles, the sound loud against the background hum of the room.

"Well, noooo," Blake said in a long drawl, his eyes searching mine. He apparently liked what he saw because he leaned forward, his lips in a taut little smile. "Babe, it can't be that different from taking on a bunch of raging demons from a hell gate."

I laughed, slapping the table, causing a couple of wine glasses to clink

together. Garret took a sip of his wine and then held it up to the light like a sommelier, examining the deep ruby color. "Blake," Garret said, choosing his words carefully. "Did you just call Sam, babe?"

I was choking from laughter while Russ looked at his younger brother in irritation. "Excuse my brother. He's still a young 'Squatch with hot blood."

"No offense," I said, turning to Blake. "First of all, I'm probably as old as your mother. Second of all, I'm happily married...to a woman. Maggie and I will be celebrating our wedding anniversary very shortly."

Blake's mouth formed an O, and he sat back, looking slightly embarrassed and thoroughly at a loss for words.

"Second of all, I'm the leader of the Silverthorn Pack. I know what a pack of werewolves defending their territory can do, and

I assure you, they can take down several Sasquatch, especially if you underestimate them."

"Right," Russ said. "Like I said, my brother Blake is an idiot. He's helped Potentia Security out with a few jobs up here in the Pacific Northwest, but he's never battled a named one or looked Lucifer dead in the eye. We also should let you know we think they have weapons. Silver bullets, to be exact."

I felt a shiver snake down my spine. The room's warmth seemed to dissipate as the gravity of his words settled in. Silver bullets were one of the few things that could kill us besides fire and old age. In fact, I had lost my mother and one of my brothers just last year in a fight with Orchium that had led to us being here. They were deadly and cold-blooded, that already knew.

"So what we are saying is that we are going to need some help, especially since Beth seems to think Orchium has made a deal with the Devil. They seem to be using the hell gates to transport drugs. This is bigger than just the Pacific Northwest," Easton said, looking sternly at Blake. His voice was steady, but the tension in his shoulders was evident.

"We are definitely going to need some help," Garret said, setting his wine glass down with a soft clink. "But there are other werewolf packs in the area."

"There are," I said. "And what I'm going to need from you, Russ, is an introduction."

"Of course," Russ said. "There are two packs in the area. We've got the Aldeen Pack to the north, right in the area we saw Orchium. They've got to know about the interlopers. And then we have the Lowell Pack to the west on Sourdough Ridge."

"I love the names around here," Garret said. "It's like the Wild Wild West."

"It still is the Wild West in some ways," Morris said, leaning back in his chair, casting a critical eye on Garret. The chair creaked under his weight, adding to the room's symphony of noises. "We are the law here. Nothing happens that we don't know about."

"Well, then, you'll be the perfect partners," Garret said, lifting his glass with a smile.

"There is just one thing…" Morris said, still keeping his eye on Garret. The firelight cast long shadows on his face. "No one likes vampires."

"Well, maybe I can change their mind," Garret said sullenly, a frown crossing his face. "But no worries. I like to keep a low profile."

"Where we go, Garret goes. He's been with Potentia Security longer than I have, and I trust him with my life," Easton said, his voice sounding dangerous. The room seemed to hold its breath for a moment, the only sound the crackling fire.

"Oh, no worries," Russ answered quickly. "My brother is just warning you, you might not always find a warm welcome, especially if you aren't with us."

"I understand," Garret said, a touch of sadness in his voice. "Why should I expect anything different?"

An awkward silence fell around the table, and Garret got up, drained his glass of wine, and left the meeting, opening the double doors with a soft creak and disappearing into the dimly lit dining room beyond.

"Sorry we offended him," Russ said, his voice low, almost lost in the ambient noise of the room. "That wasn't my intention."

Easton's mouth tightened. "I'll check in on him later. He gets a little sensitive sometimes. He doesn't leave Mt. Storm very often and is practically a part of the family. He's a loner at heart. I think this meeting made him uncomfortable. But he's a great asset with his ability to fly overhead. Not to mention, he's a loyal friend."

"In fact," I said, "we might want to send him out tomorrow morning to scout Desolate Peak. He can give us some insight on the extent of their operations."

"Good idea," Russ said. "Meanwhile, we have to work tomorrow. We each have our own territories we are supposed to cover. Blake has that area, so perhaps the two can work together."

"I'm supposed to head out to the town of Paradise," Morris said. "I can ask the tourists if they have seen anything unusual."

"And I can take you two out to meet the Lowell Pack first. I went to school with the boys, and they know me," Russ said. "But it's a rough territory, so maybe Sam and I could go on foot. Although we could take some four-by-fours, it would just take longer to get through the brush with vehicles."

"That's fine," Easton said. "I'll stay here and study their terminals. We need to figure out which gates they are using. I also want to check the missing person reports. They need blood sacrifices to open these gates. There has

to be a pattern of missing persons."

"I can get you the park systems reports of missing persons, and I can tap into the national database if that would be any help," Russ said, rubbing his chin thoughtfully. "And now that you mention it, we have had several hikers go missing in the last year." The room seemed to grow quieter as the weight of his words settled over the table, the crackling fire providing the only sound in the room.

"Well, it sounds like we have a good place to start," I said with relief, glad that our plan was coming together.

The server came in, carrying a huge tray of food, piled high with fried chicken with all the fixings. My mouth started to water, and I realized that I hadn't really had much to eat today.

"Dang, that looks good," I said as the server started to put the plates on the table.

Easton looked just as hungry. "I'll have to send a picture to Tina and the kids. They are going to be so jealous."

We laughed and dug in, our problems, for the moment, forgotten.

CHAPTER 3
SOURDOUGH RIDGE

I followed behind Russ, keeping his massive Sasquatch form in my sight. I didn't know this area, and if I lost him, I would have to rely on my wolf senses to get back to the lodge, so I paid close attention to landmarks and scents as we traveled.

These mountains were nothing like the ones at home, which were like smaller and older cousins of these behemoths. Occasionally, I would get a glimpse of Mt. Rainier through the trees, its tops still shining white with snow and ice this late in the summer.

Russ moved velvet-like through the trees, taking the trail where possible but sometimes stepping off to hide in the shadows when a hiker approached. It made for a long, cautious trip, and we made an odd pair: A huge fur-covered creature ten feet tall and a silver wolf who stood out in this environment like a sore thumb.

But I was enjoying the trip, it was rare that I traveled this far into the wilderness. Our family land in Mt. Storm was a haven, but every year, civilization got closer and closer. Russ had warned me this was no easy hike, and I was already panting from thirst after a few hours of travel through these forests.

When we stopped to rest near a spring that sprung out of the mountain rocks, I was happy. We found a clearing, and the cold water bubbled over the rocky edge, making a waterfall. Russ cupped his huge hands, taking scoops of water to his mouth. He grunted and let out a short snort, which I took to mean "drink up," and then leaned against the dark rocks, almost seamlessly camouflaged.

Approaching the water cautiously, I looked upstream and down. It wouldn't be good to run into a mountain lion or bear in these woods, even with Russ with me. Seeing it was safe, I lapped at the water, my long tongue tasting hints of the mountain's minerals.

And then we were off again, pausing only around noon to shift into our human forms and take food out of our packs.

"We are making good time. Hopefully, we reach the area by nightfall," Russ said, flipping open his dark green pack and taking out a packet of jerky.

I took a piece from him, biting into the tough meat. "It's a full moon tonight, we will find them one way or another," I said, and then took out a chocolate bar, passing him a few squares.

"You ready to spend a night in the woods?" Russ said with a grin, crossing his arms across his chest.

"Always," I said, combing my short silver locks back with my hands. "Although these woods might be a little wilder than I'm used to."

"Not to worry, you're with me. No one messes with a Wright Sasquatch," Russ said, the corners of his mouth turning up.

"Does it ever get lonely out here, Russ?" I said, cocking my head.

"It does, sometimes. As you've noticed, there aren't a lot of eligible singles looking to date a Bigfoot," he said, a shadow coming over his face. "And my brothers and I are nearly the last. There are some Sasquatch clans in the world, but we tend to stay to ourselves."

"I see," I said. "You know, I married a human, and it's worked out pretty good."

He shook his head, and I got the feeling he didn't want to talk about it anymore. Closing his bag, he looked off into the distance. "Let's get going, Sam. Times a-wastin'."

I slipped the bag back onto my shoulders, the familiar weight settling against my spine, and then dropped to all fours. A surge of raw power rippled through me, the magic twisting and coiling like a living thing, racing through my veins. I felt my bones shifting, shortening with a series of sharp, almost painful cracks, as my limbs restructured themselves.

My skin tingled and itched as coarse fur erupted across my body, spreading like wildfire until it covered me in a thick, protective coat. My face pushed forward as my skull reshaped, my nose and mouth elongating into a fierce muzzle. My teeth sharpened to deadly points, filling my mouth with a predatory edge, a low growl rumbling from deep within my chest as the transformation completed.

Every sense was heightened, the world suddenly alive with a thousand scents and sounds I couldn't fully grasp in my human form.

In front of me, Russ was undergoing his own transformation, though the process appeared almost the reverse of mine. His limbs lengthened with a powerful, sinewy grace, muscles bulging and expanding under his skin as if they were growing by the second. His jaw extended, widening as his head enlarged, giving him a massive, imposing presence.

Fur sprouted rapidly, thicker and darker than mine, covering his expanding frame until he stood towering, a true force of nature. His eyes glinted with intelligence as he completed his shift, a low rumble of power vibrating through the air.

He closed his eyes, and I wondered if it hurt him, growing so much so quickly.

But then we were off again, the claws on my paws clacking against the hard stone of the mountain as we scrambled up a steep slope, going off the path always upward.

It was sunset when I heard the first howl, and we froze in our tracks. It was a friendly greeting tinged with curiosity. "Who are you?" it asked, in a female timber. The howl came somewhere up and to my right on the ridge line. I glanced at Russ, whose eyes were hidden under his bushy eyebrows.

My haunches on the ground, I lifted my nose straight up to the sky and answered the call. My answering howl was not threatening and meant "Friend."

Russ raised his hand, in greeting or warning, I didn't know, but let out a series of rough grunts and stomped the ground two times with his bare feet.

It was answered by a curiosity of excited yips, and I jerked my head toward Russ. He gave me a wink and then started up the ridge. Curious to meet my werewolf kin, I hurried after him, scrambling up what seemed to be a well-worn path.

At the top were three large wolves, their coats and eyes bright. They approached me cautiously, and we sniffed each other in friendship. Russ held out his hand, and the larger one licked him.

Cocking my head, I watched them start down the trail and

then yip at me, demanding we follow. This time, I took the lead, following the dark wolves across the very top of the ridge.

Now, the sun was setting to the west, blazing oranges, yellows, and pinks painting the sky in a dazzling display of what the Pacific Northwest could do. The shadows in the trees were turning purple, and I already felt an evening chill creeping into my bones.

Across the ridgeline, we traversed three brown wolves, one silver wolf, and a massive Sasquatch. I saw the warm red glow of a bonfire, a group of people, looking very much like your normal everyday hikers, surrounding it.

Of course, this was a bonfire night, and the Lowell Pack had gathered to greet the moon. Already, the mother moon was starting to rise, dancing with the setting sun in a competition for the sky.

As we approached, the circle opened, and a man stood. Immediately, I knew he was the leader. He wore a work jacket with steel-toed boots. A baseball cap on his head advertised a local paper company. A cooler stood nearby, the top flipped open, and the interior filled with cans of beer.

"Russ, how are you? Who is this wolf with you?" he asked, and I immediately started to shift.

I stood in front of him and held out my hand. "I'm Sam Silverthorn, leader of the Silverthorn Pack from West Virginia. A pleasure."

He smiled, shaking my hand with a grip of steel. "Well, I'll be. I'm Jack Lowell, leader of this pack. This is my family," he said, nodding toward the people around him, who all seemed friendly. "I've heard of the Silverthorns. You all have that fancy new moonshine brand, don't ya?"

I smiled. "We do. Although I would hardly call it new. We've been running the shine for generations. Wish I could have brought you a bottle."

"Well, we've got beer," he said with a grin, and someone fished out a can and offered me one.

I looked at it for a minute, hesitating, and then I cracked it open with a nod and took a big gulp. "This sure does taste good after that long hike."

Russ laughed and took a sip of his beer. "Hadn't been out here in a while. Thought I would check in."

"Glad you did, Russ. Have a seat, join us. We were just getting ready to discuss pack business, but I'm sure you'll be interested to hear what's been happening on the east side lately," Jack said, sitting back down.

Spaces on the logs were made for us, and I sat, listening carefully and paying attention to this pack. They all were attentive and seemed well-disciplined and healthy. At nearly twenty heads, they were a large pack, and I saw a passel of children playing noisily nearby.

"First, the business. Lumber has been good this season, and we've felled a record number of trees so far. You all know that money is flowing," Jack said, adjusting the brim of his cap. "Rick and Bob are working on replanting the pine saplings, and it looks like we will be ready to move to the new parcel next season as planned."

There were a few polite claps, and I got the impression that nearly every man there worked in the lumber business. It sounded like they must own the land and work with the paper company whose hat he wore.

"Any news on these strange trains that have been running?" a man from the back spoke. "As far as I know, BNSF and the other train lines aren't supposed to be running on these lines. They were abandoned long ago."

My ears perked up, and Russ and I exchanged glances.

"No, and they are pretty short trains, with just a few cars. Strangely, they are running too fast for this area also. I tried calling the train company, and they said I must be mistaken, as these lines aren't even maintained," Jack said, scratching his head. "And with those things…"

"I think I know who these people are," Russ spoke up, jerking his head toward me. "And my friend here can maybe fill you in."

I let out a big sigh. "Orchium. Have you ever heard that name before?"

A silence covered the group like a blanket, and Jack blinked at me. "Orchium?" he said in a trembling voice. "I have heard of them. Nothing good. Big city outfit, global drug cartel?"

"The one and the same," Russ said. "You see any sign of strange wolves or demons around here?"

Jack and one of the pack members exchanged a look. "Go ahead, Kyle."

Kyle, barely out of his twenties, looked every bit the lumberjack, with his plaid shirt, worn jeans, and a small hatchet hanging from his belt. His hand trembled slightly as he ran it through his tousled blond hair, his brow furrowed in distress. His voice wavered as he began, "We were down on the cut, just before lunch. I was the feller, chainsaw in hand, taking out the trees." He paused, his eyes narrowing as if reliving the moment. "That's when I caught the scent—something foreign, not belonging to our territory. Everything stopped, the whole site. We all knew what it meant. Without a word, we dropped our tools and went on the hunt."

I nodded, a strange wolf in your territory would be cause for alarm.

"It didn't take long for us to track them, four wolves that

weren't our kin. They were in a cave that looked like some kind of old mining cave. The thing was, when we approached, they didn't even attack. They just went further in. Who knows how far those caves go? We didn't follow, and we haven't seen them again."

Russ and I exchanged glances. A mining cave; demons were known to love caves and the underground. They made a natural place to hide a hell gate. "You see any signs of those trains in that cave?" Russ asked, holding his ranger hat in his hands.

"As a matter of fact, yes. The train tracks run right up to the entrance and go down below. Like I said, we didn't investigate further, but the trains we've seen in the wild all head in that direction."

"Sounds like that's where we need to investigate," I said, thinking that it would be dicey, going into a cave with only one wizard and a handful of allies. I glazed at Russ, who seemed to be thinking the same thing.

"Listen, would you mind keeping an eye on the area?" he asked. "Sam and I need to think of a plan, and I think we should contact the Aldeen Pack to the north."

"Good luck with that," Jack said, taking a slow sip of his beer. There was a nervous laugh around the campfire, and then he said, "They don't want to do anything if it's not their idea, and they don't like to work for free, even if it's for the common good. So you had better have something good to barter or some cold hard cash to pay them."

"I know how the Aldeens are," Russ said, rubbing his chin. "We have a good working relationship with them."

"Well, better you than me, is all I have to say," Jack said, looking off to the north, where the slopes became green again. "Are you going to spend the night? You can camp here if you want."

"Yes, we'll move on in the morning," Russ said, "and then we can find the Aldeen's tomorrow."

I held my hands out to the fire as the talk turned to how dry this summer had been and the ever-present risk of forest fires in the area. The shadows grew longer, and I drank another few beers, feeling the buzz flow through me.

I shouldn't be drinking. I knew it. It was a dangerous cycle I got myself into, using alcohol to cope with my problems. After my mother and brother died, I spiraled into a bad habit of drinking every day to cope. But after Maggie called me out, I stopped.

Now, I was afraid I would fall back into my old ways. I crushed the empty can in my hand and threw it back into an empty box.

Finally, one by one, our friends slipped away, and I shifted into my wolf form as Russ shifted into his massive Sasquatch form and threw another log on the fire. It would be a long night, but our fur and the flames would keep us warm on these chilly slopes.

CHAPTER 4
WIDE AWAKE

I jolted out of sleep, instantly alert. The wind was soft on my face, with a hint of incoming rain in the darkness.

The fire was only glowing embers in the pit, and I could instantly see Russ was already awake, sitting upright. He raised a long, hairy arm and pointed across the ridge with a thick finger, letting out a soft grunt.

My eyes flicked forward, and instantly, I noticed a lone silver wolf stepping slowly across the ridge, and I smelled Junior.

A low growl rose in my throat, followed by a grunt from Russ. I rose to my four feet, feeling the coldness of the night earth under my paws. We waited as the wolf approached, my senses on high alert.

The silver wolf stopped a few feet from me. He was disheveled, his silver fur matted and dirty. Leaves and brambles were in his coat, and his blue eyes were filled with sadness.

Again, I growled, and Junior flinched back from me, fear on his face. His eyes flicked to the massive form of Russ, and I realized he was afraid of the Sasquatch.

My lips stretched wide, revealing my fangs. Eyes locked on Junior, I dared him to attack.

Instead, he began the transformation, his purple light filling the top of the ridge. Growling, I transformed as well, worried he might be carrying a gun with silver bullets.

He stood in front of me, his hands raised as I slipped into my human form seconds behind him. "I mean you no harm. I just want to talk."

I let out a chuckle. "Where are your friends? Are they going to sneak up on us like they did last time?"

Junior looked across the ridge. "No, I came alone. We're having troubles in this area due to the other packs."

"Good. I'm not in the mood for a fight," I said, rubbing the back of my neck and stretching my back. I was getting way too old to sleep on the ground in the wild.

"Why did you come? Go back home. It's too dangerous here," Junior hissed, darkness coming to his eyes.

"I've got friends," I said, nodding to Russ, still in his Sasquatch form, watching silently and dangerously.

Junior's eyes flicked to Russ. "We can take a 'Squatch."

Russ growled, and it was a terrifying sound. He squeezed his hands into fists and fixed his eyes on Junior as if daring him to make a move.

Taking a step back, panic flooded his face. "I mean, we could if we wanted. I don't want a fight, big boy. My reason for coming here is just to talk."

Suddenly, there was a howl in the distance. "The Lowell Pack," I said. "They aren't going to be happy you're in the area."

"I'll make it quick then," he said, his eyes flicking to the nearby trees. There was no way he could take an entire pack alone. "Go home. Stay out of things that don't concern you, or you're going to get hurt."

"Junior. I can't do that. This is bigger than you. Orchium is a massive organization, and they've caught the eye of the US government. No one wants this, and we will put a stop to it."

A dry chuckle emerged from Junior's lips. "You can't. You don't know what you're dealing with. Orchium is going to take over this part of the world first and then eastward. Your friends here better cooperate if they know what's good for them."

"You don't have to do this, Junior. Dad would be so disappointed in you," I said, cocking my head and looking at him. He, in fact, looked the most like our father out of all his children.

"It's too late for me. I'm in too deep. Just get out of here, Sam," Junior said, letting out a deep sigh.

"Why are you telling me all this? We know about the train," I said, hearing another howl. It didn't seem any closer. The Lowell Pack probably lived down in the valley, miles away.

He bit his lip, his eyes shifted, looking off in the distance. "Listen, I know we've had our differences, but I've made a new life with Orchium. You've exiled me. Now leave me alone. If you don't, people are going to get hurt. Your wolf friends here and these idiots," he said, jerking his thumb at Russ.

Russ stood to his full height and, with one step, reached Junior's side. My brother threw up his hands and whimpered. Russ's hands settled on his shoulders, picking him up by his jacket.

Junior's legs started kicking at him ineffectively as Russ gave him a little shake and then let out a massive roar.

It echoed off the valley, and I heard the howls again, sounding somewhat closer from the east. Our friends were on the way.

Russ threw Junior down on the ground and raised a leg as if he was going to stomp him. Junior rolled away in a haze of purple, shifting as he did so and then scrambling to his paws about ten feet away.

Without looking back, he took off down the ridgeline to the west, his tail tucked behind him and his paws digging into the dirt to gain speed. I thought for a second about pursuing him but then decided that it could be a trap. He could easily lead me to an Orchium encampment, and without backup, I wouldn't stand a chance.

An angry bellow filled the air as Russ moved forward as if to chase him. "Leave him. We can track him in the morning," I said.

Russ began to shift into his human form, and he stood in front of me, his face red with anger. "He threatened my brothers and our friends. You're just going to let him go?"

I was a little taken aback. Never had I seen Russ in such a state. Normally, he was calm and collected. "Russ, we don't know if he's telling the truth. Orchium could be camped somewhere nearby. We need to be strategic about this."

He ran a hand through his short brown hair and shook his head. "I don't like this. It sounded like a threat to me. We need to put a stop to this nonsense and..."

As he trailed off, the Lowell Pack appeared on the ridge, running straight toward us. "Well, here is our backup. Maybe we can chase him now?" I said.

Jack Lowell appeared before me in a quick shimmer of purple, his packmates surrounding him silently. "We smelled the intruder. Where is he?"

I jerked my head down the hill. "It was my brother, come to give me a warning. I think he was alone, but I can't be sure."

His eyes narrowed, and he licked his lips. "I've got a half dozen here, want to track him, at least to the edge of our territory?"

"Yes," I said, dropping to all fours. "Let's go."

Without a word, we took off, running down the ridge, the trail still fresh in our noses. Russ easily kept up with the pack, his long Sasquatch legs lopping in a light run, leaping over hedges and streams, grunting with the exertion.

We chased him for about ten miles, all the way to a river, its brim filled with fast-moving water. There, we lost the trail and took a moment to regroup as the sound of rushing waves filled the air and the light grew brighter. Morning had arrived.

"This is near the far range of our territory, and he could get out anywhere in this river. It runs near all the way to Tacoma," Jack said, his eyes scanning the water.

"Dang it," I said, glancing back at Russ, who looked calm and collected, not like he had just kept up with us miles through the forestland.

"On a good note, this is still in my ranger territory," Russ said, a slow smile coming to his face. "And we are not that far from the Aldeen Pack. We are going to need their help if what your brother said was true."

"It's about a half-day hike," Jack said. "I would go with you, but we all need to be at the worksite in a few hours, and it's been a long night. Tell them I'm in to help. We need to run these guys out of here."

"Will do, Jack. Thanks for your help and hospitality," I said, holding out my hand.

He shook it wholeheartedly, a slight smile on his lips. "From one werewolf leader to another, good luck with your brother. Family drama can really be a pain, can't it?"

"It sure can," I agreed with a sigh. "And no matter how it ends, someone isn't going to be happy with how it turns out, are they?"

"Can't make everyone happy," Jack said with a shrug. "Especially if you're trying to save the world."

With a laugh, they all turned and headed back into their territory. "Well, should we get on with it them?" I asked, looking off across the river, unsure how we were going to get across that.

"Don't worry about it. I know a better route," Russ said. "Although I'm getting hungry. Let me go try and catch some fish in the river for breakfast. I'm getting tired of camping meals."

I watched as my friend waded into the river, his Sasquatch legs firmly set in the gravel bottom. He waited, his hands just above the water, peering down. Then, with lightning reflexes, he snatched a big fish, holding it up in the air, the early morning light glinting off its rainbow-colored scales.

We rested on the rocks, eating the fish raw. I licked the blood off my snout and then approached the river to take a big cold drink from the glacier-fed lake.

The early morning run had me buzzing, and I was anxious to push onward, but Russ moved more slowly than I did, and right now, he was laying on a big rock, staring up at the treetops.

I heard the warning yip before Russ did and stiffened, looking across the river. From the trees emerged a half dozen wolves. There was a howl, but it was friendly. Glancing back at Russ, he sat up and lifted his hand in greeting.

These were obviously friends, not foes, so I watched as the pack swam across the water, making a line as they paddled.

When Russ jumped down off the rock and shifted into his human form, I followed. "It's the Aldeen Pack. They found us," Russ said softly, crossing his arms and standing on the riverbank.

"Saves us a bit of trouble," I said, biting my lip. In all honesty, I was a bit worried we had crossed paths with them at the edge of their territory. Had they seen Junior or Orchium?

In just a few minutes, they were standing in front of us, shifted and still dripping from their crossing. A huge male, obviously the leader, approached. He wore a light camo jacket with a rifle slung over his shoulder. Together, the group of people around him looked like they were out on some kind of hunting trip. Camo ruled, and I saw more weapons on their shoulders. "Russ. What are you doing out this far? It's been a while, friend."

"Leon Aldeen, it's good to see you. I'm hoping you can help us with a problem, but it's a long story. You see anything odd in your territory lately?" Russ said, holding out his hand to shake.

"No, nothing," Leon said, looking me over cautiously. "Had better things to do today than chase strays."

"I'm Sam Silverthorn, leader of my pack. We hail from West Virginia. Have you seen another silver wolf in the area this morning? That was my brother. He's gone rogue," I said, holding my gaze steady.

His eyes widened slightly in surprise. I was getting used to this reaction; it was rare for a woman to lead a pack. I noticed the subtle shift in his demeanor, a crack in his confidence. "West Virginia? Dang, you're way out of your territory."

"I am," I acknowledged. "You ever heard of Orchium?"

Leon's reaction was almost imperceptible, but I caught it—the slight stiffening of his shoulders, the fleeting glance towards Russ. It was a small shift, but telling. I could see the fear flickering in his eyes, the way his gaze darted nervously to his packmates, who in turn seemed to sense the change. They instinctively took a step back, the scent of their fear hung in the air.

"No. Never heard of them," he said, his voice betraying him. He glanced over his shoulder, his movements sharp and defensive. I sensed a forced nonchalance in his tone.

"You're afraid," Russ observed, his head tilting slightly as he studied Leon's reaction. "Why?"

Leon's face flushed. "We aren't afraid. We just know better than to go poking around in business that ain't our own."

"The reason I'm here is because of Orchium. They are moving drugs, using hell gates. My brother is working with them, and we need to put a stop to them," I said firmly.

Leon Aldeen licked his lips, confusion on his face. Finally, he sighed, his shoulders slumping. "Okay, I might know a little about Orchium. They have been moving along our northern territory and, strangely, running trains on old, abandoned lines. We had a little bit of a confrontation. They killed one of my pack mates with silver bullets. They told us that if we ignored them, they would leave us alone."

A woman in the pack stepped forward. " I'm Lettie Aldeen, if you please. It was my husband who was killed." She was young, with sad eyes and yellow hair in a braid thrown over her shoulder. She laid a hand on her stomach; she was heavily pregnant. "And this is the first pup that will be born in nearly two decades."

"So you're worried they will erase your pack," I said, nodding my head. Even my pack, a very healthy pack, didn't have many pups. We were lacking in youngsters.

"We agreed to stay out of their way and to keep outsiders out. This means you," Leon said, placing a hand on his gun. "We got some silver bullets of our own now."

"I was hoping for your help," Russ said, his voice heavy and sad.

"Can't give it to you, Russ. I'm sorry," Leon said, looking

legitimately distraught. "But you know I wouldn't hurt you or your friends if I didn't have too. Go home and take a page out of my book. Mind your own business."

"Let's go, Sam. We aren't going to get anywhere with them," Russ said sadly.

"What! What about Orchium? They're evil. We can't just let them go," I said, knowing we needed this pack's help.

Russ gave me a sharp look of warning. "Leon, I wish you and your pack well. Let's hope we don't ever have to choose sides. If we do, I hope you pick the right side."

We began walking back the way we came, and I could feel their eyes on my retreating back. Once we got out of sight, I rubbed the back of my neck. "That didn't go as planned, did it? Seems like that was a huge waste of time."

"I don't feel right about that. Something's wrong. The Leon Aldeen I know would never just let someone waltz through his territory and threaten his people like that unless he had no choice."

"You think they are holding him hostage?" I said, my voice filled with horror. I still felt like I had a target on my back and thought the Aldeens still might be watching us from the cover of the forest.

"Not him, his people. He's scared," Russ said with a sigh. "Let's head back home and see what Easton and Garret found. Maybe they have a good lead for us."

"Good idea," I said, glancing back at the path behind us. In the distance, I heard a wolf howl. It was a mournful sound, and then we both shifted and ran as fast as we could toward home.

CHAPTER 5
THE LODGE

was happy to be back at the lodge and back to civilization. The wilds of Washington weren't a good spot for cell service, that was for sure. I was anxious to check back in with Maggie and see how things were going at home.

The first thing I did when we got back was take a warm, steamy shower, rinsing the three days of trail grime down the drain. Then I took two ibuprofen, as these old bones did not appreciate living rough for that period of time.

My sore muscles were feeling better already, and I curled up on my bed on top of the comforter. When Russ and I had rolled in off the trail, everyone was here, excited to see us. Russ must have been just as tired and worn out as I was because he insisted we both needed a bit of a rest and then we would all discuss what we had been doing the past few days over dinner.

With about an hour before dinner, I pulled out my cell phone and dialed Maggie's number, feeling a hint of irritation bubble up. It wasn't like I hadn't already texted her before I left, informing her that I'd be out of contact for a few days. Yet, as usual, she answered on the first ring, her voice laced with concern.

"Hey, I was getting worried," she said, her tone a mix of relief and reprimand. I could almost hear the sigh behind her words, and it took an effort to keep my smile from faltering.

"Hey, Maggie," I said, trying to keep my voice even. It seemed like I was always having to reassure her. "I literally just got back. Three days in the forest with a Sasquatch, I don't think I'll ever recover. I shifted so many times my bones feel tired," I moaned. It was a fact. So much shifting felt like trying to do a 5K after being sedentary for years.

"Oh, babe. I'm so sorry. If you were here, I would make you some nice soup and put you to bed. Did you find out any good information?" she asked. Through the distance, I pictured her sitting on the couch in our cozy home, her feet tucked under her.

"It was at least a productive trip. I met two new werewolf packs. Very much the big, strong man type. Stereotypical alpha male wolves. One of them, the Lowells, was pretty welcoming and agreed to work with us. The other chased us out of their territory before I even set a paw on their dirt, but they were scared," I said, rubbing my eyes. It was getting dark, and I didn't have the energy to turn on a light.

"Everything's been quiet here except the distillery. We had two busloads this week! And that agreement we made with Dunn's Donuts has started. He delivered the first batch of baked goods yesterday, and we sold out."

"That's great!" I said, legitimately happy the business was clicking along without me. "And, another fact, we ran into Junior."

"In the wilderness?" she said, her voice surprised. "How did it go?"

"It was just him, he picked up me being in the Lowell

Territory. He looked terrible, and he warned us to get out of the area. I guess I should be happy he cares enough to warn me. I just wish…" I bit my lip, guilt flooding over me. I was the one who had finally exiled him. Maybe I acted too harshly.

"You did nothing wrong. Junior tried to take over the pack, and it's his fault Randy and your mom died. Don't forget. If he had never made those deals with the Devil and Orchium, he wouldn't be exiled," Maggie said, her voice getting defensive. That's what I loved about this woman. She defended me unwaveringly. It was true; I didn't always make the right decisions, but I did my best, and she knew that.

I let out a deep sigh. "You're right. I don't think there is anything I could have done different. Junior had to be exiled. He was dangerous. Still is, really."

"Be careful, love. I worry about you," Maggie said, the concern in her voice real.

"I know you do," I said. "I'll be as careful as I can. I'll be home soon. Don't worry."

After I ended the call with more promises to be safe, I lay on the bed, staring up at the ceiling. My eyes felt heavy, so I swung my legs over the edge of the bed before I drifted off to sleep. As I got older, bedtime got earlier and earlier, but six o'clock was just ridiculous.

Time to find the boys and see what they had been up to while Russ and I were gone.

▭

I found the boys on the back porch around a glass-topped table in an animated discussion. They were all there, all three Wright brothers, Easton and Garret. Easton looked up, took off his glasses, and said, "Good, she's finally here."

"Sorry, I had to call Maggie," I said, sliding into an empty, cushioned seat. I smelled dinner as I walked through the foyer. My stomach rumbled at the thought of real food after days on the trail. "What's for dinner?"

"I asked Mom to bring it out family style tonight," Russ said from the head of the table, and just then, servers bearing loaded trays came out the side door. Their trays were loaded with pork chops, mashed potatoes, and garlic green beans.

Everyone quieted as the plates were filled and beverages topped up. The outdoor fireplace was lit, and I had a pang for home as I watched the flames jump to life.

We ate for a few minutes, and then Easton spoke, "Russ filled us in on your trip. Now, let me tell you what happened while you were gone."

I wiped my mouth and took a sip of my soda. "Let's hear it, then. Hopefully, you made more headway."

Easton nodded, folding his hands on his stomach and leaning back. "I took the time to run data on the gates in this area. Just like in West Virginia, we've got mountains here galore, with lots of dark hidden, out-of-the-way spots to hide a gateway."

"And National Parks for days," I said, thinking of the remote areas stretching all around us."

"And I checked in with our Seattle office. They say that the city itself keeps them busy, so the only time they really come out to the wilderness is if they have a massive dispersal. They don't really worry about little blips."

"Sometimes they do send us to investigate," Russ said. "But by the time we get there, they are long gone. My brothers and I can't really do much, even if we find a small group, besides scare them away if we can."

Easton pulled a piece of paper from his suit pocket. It was a printed map, wrinkled and torn from use. He laid it out on the table. "While running the data, I noticed a pattern of several gates that seem to be well used—here, in the area of Mt. Fremont."

Russ glanced at it. "That was the area we were in when we ran into the Aldeen Pack," he said, his eyes flicking to me.

"And then here, north near the border of Canada. If you overlay the abandoned railway lines, you can see there is a crisscross network that stretches across the state."

I rubbed my chin as I looked in the distance. "So, it looks like they are using sets of gates for their transportation."

"It's brilliant, really," Easton said, tapping the paper. "You avoid the authorities, and these abandoned railways aren't used for a reason. Nothing for hundreds of miles besides hikers, ghost towns, and the occasional camper."

"And I flew into this area near the Canadian border," Garret said, speaking softly. "It was mostly just trees as far as the eye could see. I did explore this area more thoroughly," he said, tapping the map near Mt. Baker. "Russ asked me to check in with a Sasquatch clan there. Unfortunately, I didn't find much except an open hell gate. I couldn't see any activity, though, and I hung out there for half a day."

"Nothing?" Russ said, his forehead creasing. "It's a pretty large family, and I gave you the exact coordinates of their village."

"I found it, but it was abandoned, and it looked like the main building had been burned."

"This isn't good," Russ said. "That's a large clan, bigger than ours. They have children."

The silence fell around the table, and I realized that I hadn't ever seen any Sasquatch children, nor any female Sasquatch besides their mother.

I opened my mouth to say something and then snapped it shut. It wasn't my place, and I saw the worry on the brothers' faces.

"Should we go there?" Blake Wright said, gazing at the map. "They might need medical help, and it's not like they can go to the hospital. They are so remote."

Russ's brows furrowed as he stared into the distance, the gears turning in his mind. "We should," he finally said, his voice heavy with resolve. "They're our kin, after all. And if something's happened to the children…"

Easton's gaze flicked toward the gate, a hint of unease shadowing his features. "That gate shouldn't just be left open like that," he muttered, a slight edge in his voice. "I'm surprised the Seattle office hasn't stepped in. I'll give them a call tomorrow, see what they know."

The worry etched on their faces pulled at me. "We'll find them," I said, trying to inject confidence into my tone. "Maybe they just took off because of the gate. I'm sure they're nearby."

"I hope so," Russ said. "Without every Sasquatch child, we will die out, and the Sasquatch will walk these forests no more."

CHAPTER 6
INTO THE WILD

The Seattle office said they hadn't had time to get to the hell gate to the west. They hadn't been worried about it because it wasn't showing much activity. They were more worried about gates that kept opening in Portland. The demons that poured out possessed the homeless population and made for crime and drug use that was out of control in the city.

They were thankful when Easton offered to close the gate and offered to send us a wizard as backup. "No, I've got a team here, but thanks for the offer. We might call you in the future, though, for this big project we are working on."

We took the entire team, piling into a minivan. Garret preferred to fly, and he promised to take a path over the Mt. Fremont area to see if he could spot any activity before meeting us at the trail heading up north.

Easton slid into the driver seat, a smile on his face. He gripped the steering wheel and then lowered his black sunglasses over his face. "You ready to roll, team?" he said with a big grin.

I grabbed the armrest in the seat next to him. "These are paved roads, right?"

"For the most part," Russ said with a chuckle.

Easton reached into his jacket, and checked that he had his wand, and then he pulled away, as I fumbled for my seat belt. Not that he was a bad driver, he was just a fast driver, and he moved through traffic with speed and finesse, those years of driving for Potentia Security paying off.

We lost sight of Garret well before we reached the city. This was a three-hour drive, not counting traffic. It would have taken us days to reach on foot, and while we weren't exactly on a time crunch, it just made more sense to take a vehicle and then go into the wilds from a trailhead.

We drove through the city, and the traffic was terrible. But the sight of the Puget Sound and the ferries leaving their docks was once again beautiful. The water was wrinkled with deep blue waves, and here and there, aquatic life broke the surface. I was like a little girl, staring out the window with wide eyes as a whale broke the surface of the water and then slipped back into the dark abyss.

We drove by the Boeing factory, their murals of aircraft decorating the massive building brightly. And we saw the planes lined up, their tail fins painted brightly with foreign and domestic airlines.

Finally, as a sprinkle of rain hit the windshield of the rented vehicle, we exited the city, heading north to our destination. We arrived at the trailhead parking lot, which was mostly empty. We each took a pack filled with supplies and made sure we all had water. Who knew how long we would be out in the woods, and it was better to be prepared.

I slid the blue nylon onto my back as Easton locked up the

minivan. The Wright brothers had a serious look on their faces as they huddled together amongst themselves, whispering.

Garret appeared in the sky, circling down through the pines to land at the tree line. "It's not good, guys."

We approached, and Easton handed him a bag. "Took the liberty of throwing in a few blood bags with cold packs. Thought you would be hungry."

"Thanks," he said, unzipping the bag eagerly and taking out one of the bags. He bit into it greedily and emptied the bag in seconds.

The brothers looked away uncomfortably. This was nothing new to me. I had seen Garret do this more often than I could count. It wasn't really his fault he had been turned into a vampire against his will.

"What did you see?" Blake Wright said, with a note of disgust in his voice.

Garret neatly folded his trash and tucked it into the front pocket of the bag, his purple eyes fixing on Blake. "It doesn't look good for your kin. The houses were still empty, and I flew down and landed on one. Nothing. And the gates are still open, although I didn't see any signs of demons."

"Do you think it's a trap?" I asked Easton.

He pondered for a moment, rubbing his chin while he looked at the Wright brothers. "Maybe. We will have to be careful."

"Well, let's get on. We'll have to walk slower because of Easton unless..." Blake looked at Russ.

"We carry him? We can take turns," Russ said, looking over at the big black man.

"What? Carry me? No, no way," Easton said, his voice getting high-pitched.

"Come on. Sam had no problem keeping up with me in wolf form, and Garret probably prefers to fly anyway. I've carried your boss, Beth Potentia, on my shoulders before. You can help us travel faster because if you go on foot, you'll have to run, and we will have to stop to let you rest way too often."

I tried to hide my smile. Easton was a big man, all muscle, and probably pushing 300 pounds. I don't know if anyone had ever carried him before.

After a minute of thought, he shrugged. "If you think it's for the best."

"I do. It will take us the rest of today and most of tomorrow to get there from here in our Sasquatch form. In our human form, well, it will take us probably three or four days, depending on the trail."

"Fine," Easton said with a sigh, although he didn't look happy.

"Let's shift in the trees, just in case any hikers are nearby," Russ said, and we all moved into the cool shadows, next to Garret, who stood watching Easton with the same smile I wore.

Together, we shifted, and then three Sasquatches and a werewolf stood in the clearing. Russ was covered with dark fur, and Morris was the same color, except his scar snaked down his arm, still visible. Blake was rust colored, and he lowered himself to one knee, his big fist firmly on the ground.

Easton approached him slowly and then climbed on the big man's shoulders. It was ridiculous, really, Easton wasn't a small man, but compared to Blake's massive ten-foot-tall form, he looked tiny.

Russ gave a grunt, and then Garret said, "I'll be overhead and try to warn you if I see anything." A swirl of purple glow surrounded him as he shifted.

We took off down the path and set a fast pace. Twice, we slipped into the forest and waited quietly as a group of day hikers passed, chatting loudly and oblivious to the Sasquatch watching them pass by.

Several hours into the hike, Blake grunted and went down on one knee. Morris moved up and crouched down beside him. Easton took the cue and hopped off Blake, stretching and rolling his neck before climbing back onto Morris.

We were making fantastic time, traveling like this, and it was a beautiful day for a hike. The scent of fall was in the air, mixed with the smell of pine and the fresh outdoors. Occasionally, we could see Garret overhead through the green leaves, just beginning to be tinged with autumnal color.

We startled deer, who took off with a crash through underbrush. Squirrels overhead chattered and jumped from tree limb to tree limb as we passed.

Taking a break, we settled into a picnic area next to a stream. Changing back into our human forms to access our packs, we dug into trail mix and drank some water.

Garret joined us, his black raven feathers dark against the bright light in the clearing. A gentle breeze hit my face, and I closed my eyes to enjoy the moment. It was then that my wolf senses went on high alert, and my skin prickled in alarm.

It was a musky smell, carried on the wind, that I had smelled once before. "Orchium. Nearby," I said out loud in warning.

My friends all froze, their eyes searching the forest. "How far?" Russ asked, his eyes hooded with worry as he stood.

Facing into the wind, my nose twitched as I caught the scent of the enemy. My ears strained to pick up any sound, but there was no crashing through the brush. "One wolf, I think, somewhere to the north, in the direction we're heading. He could have been tracking us for a while; the wind just shifted."

Garret immediately launched into the air, his raven wings gleaming black against the sun. We packed up our food nervously. I noticed Easton touching his wand several times, his eyes flicking toward the brush behind us.

But as I stood still, the scent grew fainter. "Whoever it was, it's moving away," I said, tilting my nose into the wind.

"Good," Russ said. "But this worries me. We need to take cover for the night. I don't want to get snuck up on again like Junior did to us last time."

"You got any ideas? Camping in the open doesn't seem the safest at the moment, and I doubt my little single-person tent is going to be much help against a pack of angry werewolves," Easton said dryly, touching his bag.

"Yeah, this is part of the Pacific Crest Trail. Runs from Mexico all the way to Canada. Two thousand six hundred fifty miles. You've seen those little houses along the way, those are shelters. There is one we can stay at tonight."

"Just like home," I said, thinking of the Appalachian Trail that snaked through West Virginia, not far away from Mt. Storm. In the summer, the state came alive with through hikers.

"Yeah. Except our trail is a tad more dangerous," Russ said with a slow smile.

"I'm not a hiker, so I can't debate you on that," I said, shaking my head. My love for the woods ran deep, but not deep enough to travel thousands of miles on two feet and sleep in the wilderness for no good reason except to go on an adventure. I had enough adventure in my life, thank you.

"That explains the hikers then," Easton said as a large group of ten rowdy young adults came into the clearing in a rush. They looked at us suspiciously, a group of middle-aged old folks just standing around.

That is until Russ introduced him and his brothers as rangers. The girls smiled at them, and they discussed the trail at length.

With the new group of hikers, I lost the smell of Orchium completely, and it bothered me. I looked over the group and heard Russ ask where they were planning on ending their hike.

"We are planning on stopping at a dope little cabin just off the trail, about five miles ahead," a white girl with dreads said, eyeing Easton while toying with her braids.

"You mind if we hike with you folks? That's the direction we are heading, and I know the cabin you are looking for," Russ said. "It's one of the forest ranger cabins. Not technically for public use, but it's pretty much just there for winter emergencies."

"Yeah, no problem," she said. "The more the merrier!"

I wasn't sure about traveling with this group of hikers. Knowing that we would have to stay in human form would slow us down, but it would perhaps keep the wolves away. No way would Orchium want to draw attention to themselves by attacking a bunch of civilians.

After the hiking group took a short rest—which involved stretching, filling their water bottles from the stream, and readjusting their packs—we all set off together.

I still spied Garret above us, which was good, but I found myself walking by a young man who looked to be twenty at best.

"How old are you?" he asked, rubbing his scruffy beard.

"Old enough to be your granny," I said with a chuckle. "I'm from West Virginia."

"Oh, cool. I traveled through there last summer when I did the Appalachian Trail."

I looked at him more closely. Maybe he was older than I thought. "And how old are you?"

"Twenty-five," he said with a grin. "But I'm told I look younger."

I nodded, wondering what this young man did for a job and how he afforded his expensive gear. Not that I knew much about hiking, but I saw some labels that I knew were well out of my price range.

"You're probably wondering what I do for a job," he said sheepishly and then pulled out a camera. "I make hiking videos for the internet."

"Cool," I said, looking at his very expensive camera. He screwed it on a stick and then held it in front of him. I quickened my pace to get out of his shot and listened to him for a moment.

"Hey, this is Hiker Hank! We met up with a big group today, and we're all hiking together. It's been a real nice day, easy hiking, with good temperatures. My shoe is still giving me some problems, but I've duct-taped it together. Looking forward to resupplying at Stehekin, and we are going to be taking a day off, and you know I need it!"

I listened to him prattle on for a few more minutes and then put his camera away. "Fascinating," I said, cocking my head. "You have a lot of people who watch your content?"

"Millions," he said with a grin. "Although the money is really in sponsorships."

I nodded, wondering if he made more money than my successful moonshine distillery back in West Virginia, and we continued on our way. In fact, the distillery came up again, and all the young adults were shocked to learn that I owned an honest-to-goodness moonshine operation—albeit legal now.

All this conversation really took me away from the task at hand, but as we came around the corner, I got a massive whiff of wolf. I stopped in my tracks, my eyes widening. Through the trees, I saw a flash of brown, and two wolves stepped out in the path, looking toward us.

With a gasp, the entire party stopped. Easton, walking

behind me, grabbed his magic wand, and the Wrights put out their arms toward the young adults like they were concerned moms.

We all watched in silence as the wolves stared us down and then slipped back into the trees.

"That was so cool!" my new friend, Hank, said. "I got it on camera! That's my thumbnail!"

I shot a concerned look at Russ, who let out a sigh and then dropped back to me as we continued to walk. "Orchium?" he said in a low voice.

"Of course. They wanted us to see them. That was just two. There are more around," I said, my head craning behind us. I was starting to feel like we were surrounded.

"Why didn't they attack?" Russ said. "They made eye contact with us. They know what they are doing."

"These kids," I said, gesturing around us. "Can you imagine the panic if they slaughter them all? It would be national news."

"And the park service would go after them. You're right," he said, biting his lip. "The cabin isn't far. I'm glad we are staying there tonight. We will have to set a watch."

"Garret doesn't sleep; he can stay up on the roof, and then we can take turns, watching at the door all night," I said in a low voice, keeping an eye on the young adults all around us, happily traipsing down the trail without a care in the world. Young, naive, and trusting. To be young again.

Eventually, we saw the cabin through the trees. I could smell wolves all around us and even caught sight of them, just a glimpse once or twice. It was nice to open the door of the cabin and see bunks and a fireplace.

Blake opened up his medical pack and began treating the hikers' accumulated cuts, blisters, and burns. They were delighted to get even a small bit of relief after weeks of hiking.

Russ watched his brother work with a little smile on his face. "This will do. We will have to see what happens tomorrow. We will have to leave this group around midday."

Hiker Hank happily claimed a bunk, flirting shamelessly with the girl with the dreads. I hoped these young adults made it safely to their destination, deep in the heart of the Pacific Northwest.

CHAPTER 7
NIGHT VISITOR

I sat in the window opening of the cabin, the logs rough against my thighs. Behind me, I heard the rhythmic breathing of the hikers and my friends.

The moonlight fell on me, and I drew strength from the pale light. My eyes flickered to the trees, making out details the others wouldn't have seen.

In fact, I made eye contact with a brown wolf at the edge of the trees, and we sat like that, staring at each other. It was the leader of Orchium. I knew it. The sounds in the night let me know he was not alone. We were surrounded.

A rustle of wings and a flutter of black flew from the top of a tree, and the black raven landed at my side. A few moments later, Garret appeared next to me. It was a good thing he was skinny because the windowsill wasn't that big.

He lifted a long pale finger, pointing across the clearing. "They've been there all night, just watching."

My breath caught in my throat. "How many?" I whispered, careful not to disturb the sleepers.

"Four," he replied, his voice barely above a murmur. "Two broke away earlier and headed north."

A shiver ran down my spine, the weight of the night air pressing against me. The pungent scent of wolves lingered, drowning out any trace of the usual night fragrances. "Do you think they figured out we won't be easy prey?" I asked, trying to keep my voice steady despite the gnawing anxiety.

"Exactly that. But why two split off...I don't know," Garret said, drawing his knees to his chest. He looked out of place, perched like a bird in human form, his head tilting as he followed my uneasy gaze across the clearing.

"Any sign of my brother?" I asked, holding my breath.

"None. And no sign of any demons either," Garret said, resting his chin on his knees. His long, slender arms went around his legs, and I noticed a spot of blood on his sleeve.

His eyes followed mine, and he rubbed the spot. "I found two squirrels earlier and couldn't resist. All these young hikers were driving my hunger insane."

I didn't say anything to that one, glad he had satiated himself with wildlife instead of hiker blood. We sat in silence for quite a while, listening to the night sounds. An owl hooted in the distance, and the soft sounds of the tree branches rustled together in the breeze.

The sky grew darker, and black clouds covered the moon. The wind picked up, and when I looked across the clearing, the Orchium wolves were gone.

In a moment, the first raindrops hit, and both Garret and I pulled ourselves out of the window. The fresh smell of rain drifted through the opening, washing the foul smell of the wolves out of the air.

A bright flash of light lit up the bodies of the sleeping hikers, sprawled out in sleeping bags across the floor, and then the rain came harder, pounding on the roof as the cracking sound of thunder shook the cabin.

"Looks like they hightailed it out of here," Garret said, looking back out the window. Another flash of lightning outlined the sharp lines of his face, making him look paler somehow. His dark hair fell to his shoulders, slightly wavy, and lit up his purple eyes. They flicked to me and then to my empty sleeping bag.

"Why don't you get some rest? This storm isn't going to end soon, and I don't feel like flying around in the rain."

"Okay," I said, knowing my vampire friend needed no sleep. "Wake me if they come back."

Garret nodded and sat again in the window, his body dark against the flashes of lightning in the sky.

As I slid into my bag, Easton's eyes flickered open, bright white in the darkness. "Everything good?" he asked, his voice rough from sleep. I noticed he was sleeping with his wand in his hand, ready for anything.

"Yeah," I whispered. "The storm scared Orchium away."

"Doesn't mean they won't be back," Easton said, blinking his eyes against another flash of lightning. "But it sounds rough out there. Glad we have a roof." He lifted his wand, and the tip illuminated, lighting up the inside of the cabin and the sleepers lining the floor, some using their packs as pillows, others leaning against the wall.

I noticed several spots where the roof was leaking, leaving small puddles on the floor. Well, nothing could be done about that.

"Night, Easton," I said, closing my eyes, listening to the hard patter on the roof.

"Night, Sam," he said as his wand blinked out.

The next morning, I was stiffer than my momma's sheets on wash day. I groaned, feeling my age in my bones.

"Need a hand?" Easton asked with a grin, standing over me. He held out one of his massive dinner-plate-sized hands, and I took it gratefully and he hauled me to my feet.

Garret still sat in the window, but now his hood was pulled up against the morning sunlight. His hands were shoved deep in his pockets, and he watched as the young hikers rolled up their sleeping bags and headed out.

"Got to get an early start!" Hiker Hank said cheerfully, as he held his camera in one hand. Regardless of his claim, he was one of the last hikers to leave.

"Hey, Hank!" I called after him, worry filling me. "Be safe out there, okay?"

"You got it! See you old folks later! Happy trails!" he said, waving goodbye as he strutted out the door.

We took our time packing up, sidestepping the muddy puddles left on the cabin floor from the leaking roof. I dug into my pack and ate a few handfuls of trail mix while the Wright brothers stepped outside to do their business and scan the area.

Huddling near the door so that Garret could stay in the shade, we discussed our next moves.

"Lots of wolf prints around the cabin, but they seem to have cleared off," Blake Wright said, his eyes flickering around the front of the cabin.

Russ was leaning against the cabin, his ranger cap pulled low. He looked up, his face serious. "I think the storm chased them off, but we should get going before they come back."

"That's a good idea," Easton said, unfolding a topographic map. "Why don't we take the trail out this way and then follow this stream north toward Mt. Baker? The stream may help us avoid any detection from Orchium if they think we are going to be taking the trail."

"And I can fly up overhead and scout," Garret said, pulling his hood down a little farther.

I licked my finger and held it up. The wind was blowing from the west. "The wind is favorable today. They shouldn't be able to smell us coming."

"I'm worried about the Mt. Baker Sasquatches. I feel like something bad has happened," Morris said, rubbing his stubble on his chin. "We need to move fast today."

"But where are we staying tonight? I don't want to be caught out in the open. We would have been in trouble last night if we hadn't made it to this cabin," Easton said, worry crossing his face.

"I'm hoping we can stay in the village," Russ said, concern on his face. "If we can't…well, there are some sanctuary caves in the area."

"I don't know about caves," I said, sweat breaking out on my forehead, thinking of the caves around Mt. Storm. "Could be hiding a hell gate."

"Well, we are wasting time sitting here talking about it. Let's get a move on. Hopefully, we have enough time at the end of the day to find shelter," Russ said gruffly, picking up his pack.

"You lead, brother," Morris said with a little smile. "You know this area better than I."

Russ nodded, and instead of heading for the trail, he moved around the back of the cabin, and our Sasquatch friends changed one after the other. While we had traveled as humans for most of yesterday, now was the time for speed.

I dropped to all fours, feeling the morning dew under my

hands as I shifted, and then stretched, doing a down dog as my tail flicked in happiness.

With a sigh, Easton climbed on Blake's shoulders, touching his wand again to make sure he was ready.

We made straight through the trees and around the cabin. The ground and surrounding brush were still damp from the rain, and I could tell we were all going to be a muddy mess by the end of the day.

We headed through the brush for about two miles, coming to the banks of a rushing creek. Then, we turned north, following the bank as we went. Occasionally, I spotted Garret above.

Around noon, we stopped at a sandy spot and transformed back into our human forms, except for Garret, who perched on a nearby dead log and listened while we boiled water on a camp stove and then rehydrated camping meals.

I had the chili, which wasn't bad but could certainly use more spice. Our stomachs full, we took water from the stream, dropping purification tablets straight into our bottles. Easton checked his phone and frowned. "Still no service. We are so far out in the sticks we could just disappear."

"And people do," Russ said, rolling up his food package and stuffing it into the front of his bag. "Just vanish without a trace. We've been a part of so many manhunts, looking for missing hikers in the woods. Sometimes we find them, or what's left, and sometimes we don't."

"Missing 411," Blake said. "It's a real thing. Although honestly, it's mostly just inexperienced hikers who get in trouble. The animals will take care of a body real quick out here."

I shivered at the thought as we all packed up, leaving no trace. We shifted, and then we were off again, making good time. The Wright brothers took turns passing Easton around, and he good-naturedly took it in stride.

About an hour later, I halted in my tracks and let out a yip to alert the others. In the distance, I could hear a low rumbling sound, getting closer and closer by the second.

We paused, and then the Sasquatches heard it, too. Garret circled down from overhead, shifting rapidly.

"It's a train, an old, rusted-looking thing, bellowing out dirty black smoke and chugging down an old line," Garret said, alarm on his face. "I tried to get close, but I couldn't see anything out of the ordinary except..." he paused, glancing at me, "the driver."

"Not of this world?" Easton guessed, sliding off Russ's back and doing a quick stretch.

"Definitely not. It was our old friend, Sarah Morris," he said in a grave voice.

"A named one," I said with a sigh. Easton nodded. "The boss will be interested to hear of these new developments. Now, we just need to get some kind of connection."

"They are headed south, just pulling one car. I couldn't see what they were hauling," Garret said, just as we heard a train whistle in the distance.

"I want you to follow that train for a while, see where it goes. Make sure you make it back to us before nighttime," Easton ordered, pulling out his map again. He scratched his head in confusion. "There are no active tracks on this map. No idea what's happening."

Morris grunted, pointing toward his back. The Sasquatch

obviously wanted to go. So we split up, with Garret flying toward the mystery train and us toward the Sasquatch village. Soon, we would have answers, and I hoped we wouldn't get ourselves added to the missing 411 list in the process.

CHAPTER 8
THE VILLAGE

We reached the hamlet late in the afternoon, a hidden cluster of buildings nestled deep in the wilderness near the slopes of Mt. Baker. The place was so remote, it might as well have been a forgotten speck on the earth, unmarked on any map. The path to it was barely a trail, winding through the trees and thick brush.

Garret returned from scouting the train, soaring above us, only visible occasionally through the leaves.

As we neared the scattered buildings, we moved with caution, only proceeding after Garret had scouted ahead and signaled it was safe. But safety felt like a hollow word in the face of what we found.

The hamlet was a ghost of its former self. The homes, once simple shelters against the harsh wilderness, were now nothing more than charred skeletons. Blackened support beams jutted out from the heaps of smoldering rubble, like bones of some great beast slain by an unknown force. The air was thick with the acrid stench of soot and smoke, a smell that clawed at the back of my throat and made my eyes water. I wrinkled my nose, but the scent was persistent.

"Is anyone here?" Russ called out, his voice strained, cracking with the fear that none of us could fully hide. His words seemed to hang in the air, unanswered, the silence that followed more unnerving than any reply could have been.

The stillness was suffocating. The ruined buildings stood mute, offering no clues, no comfort. Even the trees, usually alive with the whispers of the forest, were eerily silent. The sense of loss was overwhelming, as if the land itself was grieving the lives that had once been lived here, now snuffed out without a trace.

It wasn't just a village that had been destroyed—it was a way of life, a small, fragile community wiped off the face of the earth, leaving nothing but ashes and a haunting feeling. It was as if something might still be lurking, just out of sight.

Morris was bent down, inspecting the dirt. "I don't see any tracks. Whenever this happened, it was before the rainstorm."

Easton was stoic, but I noticed him looking at a child's tricycle, bent and discarded near the edge of the building. His Adam's apple bobbed, and he touched the bridge of his sunglasses with shaking hands, pushing them back on his face. Glancing up at me, he said. "They aren't here, are they?"

I lifted my nose, and I didn't smell any Sasquatch, dead or alive. But then… "To the north," I said, pointing out of the town. "I smell death."

Russ swore, shaking his head. "No. They can't be gone."

"The gate is north. I suspect we will find them near the gate. I didn't spy any bodies, but it is in a clearing," Garret said.

"We have a few hours of daylight left. Let's get this gate closed and see if we can find any survivors," Russ said, his voice tight and strained.

We left the little village behind, and I felt an impending sense of dread as we picked our way north through the trees. It wasn't long before we found the first Sasquatch body just off the path, charred beyond recognition. Twenty feet later, we found two more.

"Demons," Russ said. "They're gone. All gone. Our friends."

"We'll have to give them a proper send-off," Blake said sadly, bending down and touching the body gently. He rolled the body over, and I nearly gagged from the decomposition. These bodies had been here a while.

A faint red shimmer glowed just up head, and Garret landed in the path in front of us, his eyes haunted. "There are a few bodies by the gate. They were hidden by the grass, making them hard to see from above," he said in a haunted whisper.

We edged forward, afraid of what we would find but having no other option. Easton took a device out of his pack. It looked like a radio car controller with a big knob and an antenna. Licking his lips, he stared at the gate, coming ever closer.

An old, abandoned train track appeared to our right, and I realized the line curved in front of us, eventually ending right at the gate.

Or rather, the tracks went through the gate, ending somewhere in hell?

The bodies were indeed hiding in the grass, and Russ and his brothers moved around the clearing, marking where the bodies were, while Easton, Garret, and I approached the gate.

It was just like I remembered, and I shuddered. My trip to hell and back had been anything but fun and games. The heat rolled out of the opening, formed from what appeared to be an old arch made from railroad ties.

A rusted sign hanging from one chain read YARD, and I suspected that long ago, this used to be a place to store trains.

Branching side lines confirmed that hypothesis. A rusted water tower stood to the side, nearly obscured by overgrowth.

The heat emanating from the gate blasted my face, and through the red mist, I could almost make out shadowy forms and figures on the other side. It was like I was looking through a very dirty window in a smoke-filled bar. Gulping, I raised a hand to shield my eyes from the heat.

"I'll close this up now," Easton said, holding up the portal device. He pushed the button and began to turn the dial when suddenly, a massive rumble shook the ground we were standing on.

I was standing right in front of the gate, and my eyes went wide. It was a train. The light on its front broke through the gate at the same time as the sharp, pointy cowcatcher.

"Run!" I shouted, diving to the right. My friends scattered, and I felt the whoosh of air past my face and the loud clatter of the wheels on the old track. Garret performed an almost perfect somersault and roll, landing on his feet ten paces away with his hands raised in fists.

Looking up, I caught sight of it, roaring down the lines at top speed. A massive engine, rusted and belching smoke, pulling a box car. On the top of the car were demons, and they pointed at us and laughed.

From the front of the box car, a wolf appeared, brown and massive. "Orchium," I said out loud.

The werewolf stood, his eyes narrowing as the train rumbled past, but making no move to jump off the car. He blinked, and then, in seconds, the train disappeared into the forest.

"Shit. That was intense," Easton said, scrambling to his feet. He picked up the portal device from where it had fallen. "Let's get this thing closed."

"Can't they just open it again?" Russ asked, his eyes flicking back to where the train had disappeared. "Yeah, they can. But it'll be closed for now," Easton said, twisting the knob with a determined grip. After several tense turns, the gate finally closed with a sharp snap, and we all exhaled in unison, the tension releasing just slightly. My chest loosened, but not entirely.

"If I had to guess, that's why they killed the Sasquatch. Their village was too close to whatever this is," Easton continued, but his words barely registered.

I glanced at the sky, feeling the weight of the encroaching darkness press down on me, a tightness forming in my chest. "It's getting dark," I said, my voice thin as the worry coiled in my stomach.

"There's a sanctuary cave nearby," Russ said, his voice steady but his eyes betraying a hint of the same unease. "Our ancestors used it to hide in times of trouble. If there are any survivors, that's where they'll be. I hope we find someone."

My heart pounded in my chest, the dread seeping into my limbs, making them feel heavy. I could feel the tension in my shoulders, the gnawing anxiety refusing to let go.

He set off toward the west, and we followed. Garret walked behind me, cursing about tree roots and blood-sucking bugs, which I thought was ironic.

Easton walked in front of me, unmoving. He was ex-military and had spent time in survival situations. This little slice of the wilderness didn't faze him, even if brambles sometimes caught his jacket. He brushed them away casually.

I longed to shift into my werewolf form, but as the Sasquatch were still in human form, I followed their lead. They knew this area much better than I did.

A hillside rose out of the brush, one of the many rocky outcroppings that dotted this wild and inhospitable part of the world. A stream trickled to the right, fed by the surrounding peaks.

There was even a path here, well worn. As we neared the cliff face, I heard a strange sound. It sounded like crying. "Up ahead!" I said with alarm. "I think it's a child."

Russ nodded and called out. "Are you there? It's me. Russ Wright, of the Wright Sasquatches. I'm a friend."

The sound went silent. In fact, the entire forest was eerily quiet, as if holding its breath. And then, there was a small voice. "I remember you. You're that forest ranger. Please come, Angela is hurt bad, and it's just us kids."

From the tree line, a small figure stepped out of the shadows. It was a girl child with a tear-streaked face. She was wearing a calico dress that looked like it was straight out of the Wild West, and she didn't have shoes. She was holding a blue pail dripping with stream water.

Russ dropped to one knee and shimmered. His brothers followed suit, and soon, all three Sasquatches took up the trail.

The little girl smiled, shifting with them and then holding out her arms. She was a child Sasquatch, a little version of Russ and his brothers. Her fur was black, and her eyes a bright blue, still filled with tears.

Russ lifted her up, carrying her on his waist, with one arm wrapped around her shoulders. He glanced back at us, a signal for us to follow. I picked up the pail of water. At least I could be helpful.

We approached the cave, and Russ and his brothers let out a series of loud grunts. Little child grunts answered, and Russ put down the girl and then disappeared into the cave with his brothers.

Easton, Garret, and I waited outside, unsure if we should follow. But we didn't have to wait long. Russ appeared out of the cave with blood on his hands.

"Easton. I need you. We have a hurt Sasquatch inside. You two, come also."

Easton grabbed his wand, and we entered the cave. It was narrow at the entrance, widening at the back. I could see a half dozen small Sasquatches, their eyes terrified. Bedrolls and discarded blankets lined the floors, along with a few stuffed animals.

In the middle of it all was an adult female Sasquatch, horribly injured. Second and third-degree burns covered her chest, and half of her fur was missing. Blake was at her side, his bag opened, but he had a helpless look on his face.

Not only that but her arms were covered in deep bite marks. She lifted her head and stared at me, her nose widening.

"I told her that you were a werewolf but a friend. Angela saved the children by moving them here. She tried to go back to help the others but was attacked. Can you help her?" Blake asked, leaning down and taking one of her hands gently. "There isn't much more I can do besides make her comfortable before she passes."

"Can she shift back into human form? I'm not sure how my magic will work on a Sasquatch?" Easton said, getting to his knees across from Blake.

In response, she shifted and as she did so, let out a gasp. In her human form, she was wearing a shirt hanging in charred strips. Her arms looked terrible, more like hamburger meat.

"Please. Help the children. Get them to safety," she said in a weak voice. "I saved them. It was all I could do."

"You did a good job. And don't worry, you're coming with us," Russ said, squeezing her hand.

"It hurts. All over," she gasped, her back arching.

"Your Sasquatch body was stronger. Easton, hurry!" Russ's voice was filled with panic.

Meanwhile, Morris was behind us, comforting the six children. He took the smaller ones in his arms while the older ones buried their faces in his thick fur.

Easton pulled out his wand and held it over her. His other hand moved, palm down, over her chest. His hand glowed with magic, and he swept it over her body.

I had been blessed to have been healed by magic before and knew the exact feeling. It felt wonderful, like a jolt of power. Any broken bones would be mended, burns healed, aches receded. The only things a wizard's magic couldn't heal were cancers and dementia, as I knew well from my own wife's bout of breast cancer.

I had nearly lost Maggie, and it was only by turning her into a werewolf I could save her. Every day, I was glad of her second chance.

But these Sasquatches wouldn't be happy to be turned into a werewolf if that was even possible. I watched her blue eyes widen and then soften as the pain receded.

Finally, she was still and breathing. Easton offered her a hand, which she took, sitting up gingerly.

"You healed me," she said with wonder. Her hand rubbed across her chest, exposed now, the burns gone. I dug around in my pack, finding my one extra shirt.

"It's not clean, but here," I said, passing it to her.

She put it on, a smile coming to her face. One by one, the children shifted. They were all dressed in the same strange Western clothing.

"Angela! Angela! You're all better!" They clung to her, their faces upturned and shining. One small boy, his eyes brimming with unshed tears, asked, "Can that man heal our mommy and daddy too?"

Angela's smile crumbled, replaced by a look of such profound sorrow that it seemed to age her instantly. She knelt, gathering the children close, her voice thick with emotion. "Oh, my darlings," she whispered, her words catching in her throat. She took a deep, shuddering breath, tears spilling down her cheeks. "I'm so, so sorry, children. They... they are gone. No magic, no matter how powerful, can bring them back to us."

The children's smiles fell, confusion and disbelief filling their faces. Angela held them tighter, her body shaking with silent sobs as the full weight of their loss crashed over them.

Russ watched the scene unfold, his own heart heavy. After a moment, he stepped forward, his voice gentle but urgent. "Angela," he said softly, "I know this is difficult, but we need to understand. Tell us what happened. How did the entire village fall?"

Angela looked up at him, her eyes red-rimmed and haunted. She nodded slowly, steeling herself to relive the horror. She stood up, shakily at first.

"Take it easy," Easton warned, steadying her with a firm hand. "You need to rest."

"I need a drink of water first," she said, touching her dry lips.

"Fresh from the stream," I said, passing her the blue bucket. She took it in both hands, taking a deep drink.

She sighed, wiping her mouth with the back of her hand. "They attacked in the middle of the night three days ago. The gate opened, and the demons came roaring out. I had just enough time to take the children and hide them here in the cave.

I told them to stay put, and then I turned to head back to defend the village. I didn't make it twenty steps away when the demons and those wolves attacked me. They left me for dead, but I crawled back. There are no others?"

"No, everyone is gone. We need to lay them to rest," Morris said, shaking his head.

"That's what little Rebecca here reported. She snuck back to the village yesterday. I wish she didn't have to see that," Angela said, and little Rebecca, the girl we had found crying outside, rushed to her and gave her a hug.

"We can't stay here. The gate will reopen. If not today, then sometime soon, although time in hell runs differently. One minute in hell is one week outside. So it could be weeks before they can reopen it," I said, chewing on the inside of my cheek. I felt like a sitting duck here, just waiting for the hordes of demons to arrive.

"As soon as we get in cell phone range, I'll notify the Seattle office. It's possible they may want to send out government forces to secure the area. There is something strange going on here," Easton said. "We've never seen trains being used before. We need to find out where they are going."

"We do. But the first thing we need to do is get these children back to the lodge. My mom will know how to take care of them," Russ said, looking at Angela. "Will you come back with us?"

"I don't have much choice, do I?" she said quietly. "We can't stay here. Everything is gone."

"Don't worry, you always have a home with the Wright Sasquatches," Russ said. "We're practically family."

"Thank you," she said. "Now it's time for dinner. Luckily, we kept this cave stocked with canned goods. It's not much, but I hope you can join us."

"Sure, and we have some lovely camping meals to add to the potluck," I said with a smile, thinking of our potlucks at home. We never had much, but we always shared. Just like these folks. I felt sorrow for these children, who had lost so much but now looked at us shyly with hope on their tear-stained faces.

CHAPTER 9
FLEE

At first light, Russ and his brothers buried the bodies in a mass grave. We all gathered while Blake placed a large rock on the mound to mark the spot.

It was a solemn moment, a sign that this little Sasquatch hamlet was no more. The children cried, then placed small bundles of wildflowers—gathered at our direction to keep them occupied—on the mound, where the bodies of their loved ones lay.

After the little funeral, we began to make our way back slowly, as we had six children with us, not to mention Angela, who, although healed, didn't have the stamina of the rest of us.

Russ held out his hand to her as we scrambled up a rocky ridge. "Are you okay?"

"I'm fine," she huffed, pulling her hand back. "You don't have to baby me."

We were traveling in human form just because we were a big group. Easton talked and laughed with the children, anything to keep them occupied and their minds off their grief.

I looked up. Garret was swirling down from the sky. I

paused for a moment, and he landed on my shoulder, fluttering his feathers.

"All clear?" I asked, and he nodded then sprang back into the air again to keep watch.

"Why does your raven never make a sound?" a little girl asked as she walked beside me.

"He's shy," I said, shading my eyes and watching him disappear to the south.

"Robbie!" Angela called out sharply to one of the young boys as he scrambled into the underbrush, his eyes fixed on a patch of berries. "You need to stick with us!" The boy sullenly rejoined us, and Easton chuckled, handing the small boy over his bag of trail mix, which he happily shared with the others.

I wasn't just worried about the children being underfoot; I was also concerned about the Aldeens being furious that we were trespassing on their territory, or Orchium stalking us like they had on the way there.

The trees stood still, their branches unmoving. Not a single leaf rustled, and the usual chorus of chirping birds and rustling underbrush was absent. Even the air felt heavy, thick with anticipation.

"I can't wait until we get back to the lodge," Easton said, wiping the sweat off his dark skin with the back of his hand. "I can contact Beth right away and get more resources in this area."

My voice lowered, as I didn't want Angela or the children to hear what I had to say. "I'm worried, Easton. I feel like we are being watched."

"I know," Easton said, his eyes flicking behind us. "It doesn't feel right, does it?"

"They slaughtered the Sasquatch village. It's obvious Orchium doesn't want witnesses. I keep waiting for an attack."

"Yet none comes. We will have to pick our camping spot

tonight carefully. Maybe we can find another cabin," Easton said, looking behind us at the children, now sharing the bag of trail mix.

"I didn't really expect this to turn into a rescue mission," I said, biting my lip. "But we've got to get these children to safety before we go poking the bee's nest."

"Yes," Easton said and then fell back, letting me pass. One of the smaller children was walking slowly, her head down. "Hey, you want a piggyback ride?"

The child's face brightened immediately. "Yes, please!" she said, holding her hands out. Easton swung her up on his shoulders effortlessly, and she giggled.

Russ noticed and picked up another child that was walking slowly. Angela started singing a hiking song, filling the quiet woods with sound.

As our moods lightened, Garret checked in on us, landing on my shoulder. His beady raven eyes were bright, and he clicked his beak and gave me a little nod that meant all was well before taking wing again.

It was about an hour until darkness when Garret returned. He landed in front of us, transforming into his human form for the first time today. I could tell he was hungry; his eyes were deep set, with dark circles around them, and he looked gaunt and tired. "I didn't find any shelter, but there is a natural box canyon just off the path here," he said, pointing to the west.

"Lead the way." I was glad he had found somewhere suitable.

Garret looked up at the last remaining light and pulled up his hood. With a deep sigh, he stepped off the path, leading the way deeper into the woods.

The box canyon he found was perfect. One entrance, surrounded by rocky steep sides, with the roots of pine trees knotted above us. It was narrow at the front, widening slightly as it opened. It would be a tight fit, but our body heat would keep each other warm.

The ground here was sandy, and we crossed over a downed log, with a rushing stream under us, to reach it.

"This will work. Garret, why don't you go take a breather. We'll be fine for a bit," I said, and he looked at me thankfully, quickly slipping into the trees to hunt for his dinner.

"Morris and I will see if we can find anything for us," Blake said while Morris put down a small child and his pack.

Angela gathered the children around her. All six faces looked up at her with trust. "Okay, children, I'm going to need you all to go find some wood for the fire by the stream."

They rushed off, glad for a chore to do, but stayed within eyesight.

Angela sat down heavily on a rock, putting her head in her hands. "I'm so tired."

"You need to rest," Russ said, sitting next to her. He took off his forest service jacket and placed it around her shoulders. She smiled up at him gratefully, zipping up the jacket.

"Do you think we'll be safe tonight?" she said, her eyes filled with fear.

Russ glanced at me, worry on his own face. "I hope so."

"Garret and I will keep watch," I said, leaning down to touch my toes to stretch out my calves.

"Don't forget me," Easton said. He was crouched down, rummaging through his pack, pulling out his collapsible hiking pot to boil water.

Soon, the kids came back with more than enough firewood for our purposes. Easton winked at the children, pulling his wand out with a flourish. "One of the benefits of having magic is I don't need flint and steel to start our fire."

The children giggled as the logs ignited, and we all gathered around the crackling flames as the sun went down.

The sky turned pink and red in the distance, and the soft sound of cicadas filled the air as the fire warmed us.

Morris and Blake came back, slapping four fat salmon on a flat stone. "Just have to clean these up," Morris said, pulling out a rather large hunting knife.

"Fish? I was expecting deer or something?" I said, glancing at Russ, who stood nearby, sharpening sticks to roast the fish.

"Believe it or not, fish are easy for us Sasquatch to catch. You ever see a nature documentary with a bear grabbing salmon out of the river?"

"Yeah?" I said, my mind drifting back to Sunday nights of my childhood. My family and I would gather around our little television set in the main room, while Mom popped big bowls of popcorn. In the backwoods of West Virginia, PBS and the science show NOVA were among the few programs we could reliably watch.

"Well, it's the same thing, basically. The fish practically come to us," he said, taking the clean fish from the rock and stabbing it with the pointed stick.

Soon, the fish was roasting over the fire, and Angela took out some of the provisions she had brought from the Sasquatch cave, making some tea for us all with the boiled water.

It was pleasant here, sitting on the still-warm rocks. But I saw the sadness on the children's faces now that the adventure of our hike was over. They huddled around Angela, resting their heads on her lap or hugging her legs.

We ate as the sun disappeared below the horizon. Garret set

up against the canyon walls, his arms crossed and his eyes closed. It looked like he was sleeping, but I knew he was very awake.

After we ate, picking the hot fish off the wooden skewers with our fingers, Russ kicked out the fire so we wouldn't be a beacon in the darkness.

Our group settled in for the evening. Our fur would keep us shifters warm. Easton zipped up his jacket and sat down next to Garret with his wand in his hand. His eyes got heavy, and his chin dropped to his chest. Soon, my massive friend was snoring heavily.

"I'll take watch. Get some sleep," Garret said, never moving from his spot.

We all huddled together in the canyon, mostly to keep warm. Curled up on my back were two Sasquatch children.

Angela began to hum, low and melodic. Russ, Blake, and Morris joined her in a strange song I didn't understand. I could feel the sounds vibrating in my chest.

Whether it was the low, rhythmic humming or the sheer weight of my exhaustion, I eventually drifted off. But sleep offered no escape. My dreams twisted with unease, filled with shadowy figures and the echo of distant howls. The image of my brother kept slipping through my grasp, always just out of reach, as the presence of the Orchium wolves loomed closer, a constant, suffocating dread that refused to let me truly rest.

***

I woke to the warmth of sunlight on my face and the rich aroma of coffee drifting through the air. Blinking against the light, I shifted and found Russ already up, sipping from a steaming mug.

"You should have woken me," I said, stretching the sleep from my limbs.

Russ shook his head, offering a small smile. "You needed the rest. Besides, we'll need you sharp for scouting today."

Easton glanced up from his paper map, his brow furrowed in concentration. "We're heading straight through Aldeen territory," he said, tracing a path with his finger. "But the good news is, we should be back in friendly territory by tomorrow."

"Man, I'm going to be glad to see a real bed," I said, stretching out my back. "I don't know how you rangers do it, day in and day out."

"You get used to it," Russ said, glancing at Angela, who was braiding her hair back into a long plait.

"I think we'll make better time if we all travel as Sasquatches," she said, keeping her head down.

Russ rubbed his chin, looking over at Easton. "We would have to stay off the main paths to avoid hikers and go straight across some rough territory."

"Whatever you think best," she said, but I could tell she didn't agree with the slower option.

Russ thought for a moment, looking at us all gathered around. "Easton, can you keep up? You can follow behind us, so we will all break the path for you."

"Yeah," he said, looking nonplussed. "I got a good night's sleep. Plus, I can keep an eye on these troublemakers." His voice was full of warmth, and he reached over and tousled a young Sasquatches' hair.

"Let's go then. Easton, you give a holler if you need a rest," Russ said, shifting in a shimmer of purple into his Sasquatch form.

Soon, we were all cutting through the forest in our real

forms. Garret stayed with us, perched on Easton's shoulder, as it was too hard for him to track us through the heavy foliage.

And indeed, we made good time, snaking through the forest in a line. Four adult Sasquatches led the way, with six little furry children scrambling behind. I padded alongside Russ and Angela near the front, my sharp wolf senses scanning the forest ahead.

We stopped at noon, briefly, for a snack and rest, and I noticed the storm clouds moving in. "It looks like another storm," I said, smelling the scent of rain on the breeze. "We are going to get wet."

"We still have the river to cross," Easton said, looking at his map again. "With all the rain we've had, I think we should take the pedestrian bridge marked here on the map. The river is going to be full and fast."

"That's not a bad idea," Russ said, examining the map, his finger following the topographic lines. "This river is a killer. A few people die every season, trying to cross it when it's high."

And then I caught the scent of a werewolf. My eyes flicked to the forest line. "We've got to go, NOW," I said, a note of urgency in my voice. "There are werewolves in the area."

We all jumped up and moved forward as a light rain started to fall, and I was glad for it. It would hide our smell, wash it away, and make us harder to track. But in the distance, I heard a wolf howl, and my ears stood up on alert. They were tracking us.

The Sasquatch must have heard it too, as our pace quickened to nearly a jog. Easton somehow managed to keep up, running alongside the children and matching the fast stride of the Sasquatch.

And then the rain came down harder, and we were all soaked.

The Sasquatch feet left massive, platter-sized footprints in the mud, with the smaller footprints following. So much for hiding our route. Easton was now covered with mud. Even Garret, on his shoulder, looked miserable, his feathers wet and his head hanging.

We reached the bridge, and I was glad we had decided to come this way. Under the wood span, the river raged, white waters swirling dangerously around massive boulders the size of cars.

We set off, the wooden bridge groaning under our combined weight. But we made it to the other side without incident. The Sasquatch children viewed it as an adventure, but only I knew how much closer by the minute the wolves were getting.

I looked back as we took off and saw a flash of brown in the trees. I howled urgently, and Easton looked back. "There they are! Let's go!"

Three wolves emerged from the trees and approached the crossing. I raised my nose in the air. Orchium wolves. This was interesting, and more danger than I was prepared for. Frankly, I would have preferred meeting the Aldeen wolves again. At least they seemed reasonable.

Easton pulled out his wand, which leaped to life in his hand. He pointed it at the crossing, and a brilliant ray of light shot from the ruby-tipped wand, striking the wooden bridge. After a moment, it began to smoke and then burst into flames. The fire spread rapidly, with bright orange and yellow flames licking up the sides of the bridge, crackling and roaring as they consumed the wood. The heat was intense, radiating outward and creating a stark contrast to the cool rain.

Droplets of rain sizzled as they hit the flames, sending up small puffs of steam. The heat from the fire made my face feel flushed and dry, while the rain provided brief, cool relief as it trickled down my skin. Easton's face was a mix of determination and intensity, his eyes focused and narrowed as he watched the flames take hold

The wolves that had been approaching backed off and then, with a series of yips, turned and sprinted to the north. They were most definitely heading for another crossing.

We didn't wait and took off at a full run. I had no idea where we were heading, but we just kept going. My breath hitched in my side, and I knew Easton had to be hurting, but he kept running like a machine. He was in really good shape for a man his age.

Finally, after what seemed like hours of running and the sound of howls in the distance, an ominous rock formation appeared in the distance. It was basalt stone, dark and craggy. The rain stopped, but everything was still wet.

The mysterious rocks glistened in the distance. Whatever was waiting for us there, we were headed straight for it.

CHAPTER 10
THE STAND

We reached the rock, rising out of the forest like a fortress. We neared the face, and Russ pointed out a very narrow path that snaked up the side. He grunted, looking at me with his black eyes.

Angela and the children went first, and for such massive creatures, they scrambled up the muddy slope with no problem.

Garret hopped off my shoulder, gave his black wings a few shakes, and then glared at me. Spreading his wings, he hopped into the air, his wings beating as he rose straight up the cliff face to the top. Then, he appeared in his vampire form, his deep black hood shading his face. He looked down, grinning at us, as we began to climb up, slipping and sliding.

As we traversed the path, I noticed strange markings on the side of the cliff. Pictographs scratched into the hard granite. I could make out large creatures, that were probably Sasquatch, hunting deer and other animals.

It was rough art, but I wondered if any scientist had ever studied it. My attention was broken as we neared the top.

Here, it was windy and flat. Stacks of boulders were piled at the edge, as well as some huge logs and sticks, which must have been hauled up here from below.

Easton pulled out his cell phone. "Think maybe I'll get cell service up here?"

"Maybe," I said, scanning the horizon. Not that I could see any cell towers, but perhaps with the height he could get some bars.

Angela shifted. She knelt, drawing the little ones close. "Children, you know this place. This is one of our sacred sites, a place of protection. It's called Sasquatch Hill. Our ancestors have come here for generations to hide in times of danger."

Garret cracked his knuckles, looking over the edge. "They are coming, and I'm ready for a good fight today."

"Yeah! I got bars!" Easton said. "It's weak, but I'm going to try to call Beth, see if we can get the Seattle office up here with more resources."

I looked around. There was nothing up here but an old, blackened fire pit and piles of rocks. "I don't see much up here that's going to be useful to defend ourselves."

"Oh, but you don't know where to look," Angela said, looking down at the ground. She moved a few feet away from the charred fire pit and then picked up a large rock, revealing a trap door set in the ground. Grimacing, she grabbed the handle with both hands, and it came open with a lurch. Inside were cans of food and water, matches in a plastic box, and what looked like a stash of rock slings.

"Boys!" Angela called out. "Who wants a sling?"

Morris, Blake, and Russ grunted, and she passed several to them. The weapon looked comical in their massive fists.

"Children, you each take one, but you are going to stay over here, to the right. Gather your rocks and stay away from the path."

I could see it was the only way up. This hill was easy to defend, which was good because, from below, I heard a series of howls. "They're here," I said, looking back at Easton, who was on his cell phone a few feet away.

"We are at 46.59'56.9 N and 121.45'13.3 W," Easton said, his voice choppy. "It's developing into a dangerous situation; we could use some backup from the local office."

"Sasquatch Hill," Angela piped in as Russ and Morris each picked up one end of a log and approached the edge of the trail. I shifted, moving closer to the edge, and looked over.

I was shocked to find that Sasquatch Hill was surrounded by nearly fifty wolves, all brown-furred, except for one. My brother, his silver fur shining in the light, paced at the bottom. Next to him was a large wolf, which I recognized as the leader of Orchium. *Looks like the whole gang is here.* I thought to myself. A snarl rose in my throat, and I let it loose just to warn those bastards below I was there.

"Confirmed. We have six Sasquatch children here and four Sasquatch adults. One werewolf, one vampire, and myself. We are surrounded but in a well-defended position. Looks like about…fifty angry wolves. We can hold out until the cavalry gets here, I think," Easton said, pulling out his wand.

I heard the distant, tinny voice of Beth Potentia, head of Potentia Security, protector of the world from the gates of hell, and defender of all paranormal and cryptid spirits, come through Easton's phone. "Hang tight, team. I'll get you a backup and extraction."

Seconds later, I saw Russ and Morris drop the first log. With a crash, it went tumbling down the hill, clattering and shattering into a hail of dangerous splinters on the way down.

Russ roared, beating his chest. Morris joined him and then the others, the guttural sounds filling the air menacingly.

Easton stood casually on the edge and lifted his wand. The tip glowed with an orb of pure orange, growing larger and larger. Then, with a flick of his wrist, it went flying down the side of the mountain, hitting Junior on his right flank and setting him ablaze.

"Save some for me," Garret said, never taking his eyes off the pack. Junior yelped and then rolled on the ground, quickly putting out the magical flames.

But then, the sound of fifty snarling wolves rent the air, and the pack leaped forward, scrambling up the side of the hill.

Instantly, the rocks started to fly out of the slingshots, hitting their targets true. I watched several wolves fall, their heads bleeding.

Garret stood at my side at the very top, waiting for the first enemies to arrive, but the Sasquatch defended the hill so well it was several minutes before the first wave reached us.

A brown wolf came charging straight toward me, and I felt my haunches tighten automatically. I launched at him, my jaws snapping. We hit each other solidly, still in the air, and I twisted as I got a mouth full of fur.

To the right of me, Garret had his arms around a werewolf, dragging him toward the edge. The wolf snapped at him but was unable to get purchase on my nearly impenetrable vampire friend. I heard a snap, and then Garret let the wolf drop. He had broken its neck.

Meanwhile, I was rolling with my opponent, twisting and scrambling on the ground. There were wolves all around me, and in a flash, I saw the Sasquatch adults had backed up to the other end and were defending the children.

I felt a bite on my shoulder, and my vision became blind with anger. A roar clawed its way out of my throat, and with a surge of adrenaline I managed to twist out from under my attacker.

We circled each other warily. Waiting for him to make the first move, I saw more wolves arriving at the top of the trail.

Easton was there, his hands held upright. A wave of fire swept over them, pushing them back away from the edge.

And then my opponent launched, but I was ready for him. I jumped up, throwing him off course. My front claws dug into his soft underbelly, and I felt my enemy's warm blood wash over me like a river.

"They are coming!" Easton yelled, pointing to the west. Then, another wave of wolves emerged, and the sharp crack of lightning emerged out of his wand, hitting the wolves and throwing them to the sides, where their bodies fell limp.

Two black specks appeared in the distance—large military helicopters flying low over the trees.

At first, the distant thudding sound was barely audible over the sound of Sasquatch grunts, werewolf howls, and the sizzle of magic, but as moments passed, the rhythmic beating became more pronounced.

A low-frequency thump echoed through the air as the black specks became larger. I could see men in military garb crouched and waiting to join the fight.

"It's the Wizard Corps!" Easton said, punching the air. "My old unit!"

I grinned, remembering that Easton had served for many years in the US special magical forces, using his magic to defend the country, both here on our soil and in the depths of hell.

The silhouette of a military helicopter was unmistakable. The rotating blades sliced through the air, creating a distinctive "whop-whop" noise that reverberated through the surroundings.

The low rumble of the engine accompanied the rhythmic beat, and the wolves paused for a moment, regrouping at the bottom of the hill.

As the helicopter approached, the ground beneath me seemed to vibrate in sync with the powerful thrum of the engine. The mechanical symphony grew louder, and we moved back to the edge of the hill as the two aircraft descended gracefully.

Military folk swarmed out, all holding thick, powerful-looking wands. They quickly moved to the edge of the hill, taking over the fight and swiftly joining the Wright brothers, who had resumed slinging rocks and throwing down logs now that the wolves had momentarily retreated.

It was overwhelming, the sound of the helicopters and the heat of two dozen fireballs being thrown down the hill all at once. A leader approached Easton. "I'm Captain Townsend, wizard brigade. Give me a quick rundown."

Easton spoke quickly, giving him the situation in as few words as possible, "They attacked the Sasquatch village to the north, near Mt. Baker. We are in the area to investigate Orchium, on Potentia Security business. We didn't expect to run into a village of Sasquatch in distress. Orchium destroyed the village, and these are the survivors. We are trying to make it back to the Wright Lodge, but these wolves have been trailing us the entire way."

"We will evacuate the survivors and then secure the area. I'm going to need these 'Squatch to shift!" the Captain barked over the sound of the fighting and machines.

Easton nodded and then approached Angela, who quickly shifted into her human form, followed by the children. Russ approached, looking at her carefully.

"Don't worry, I'll get the children to safety," Angela said. "Are you coming?"

Russ shook his head, touching her hand, concern deeply etched in his Sasquatch face. He gave out a low grunt, and she nodded.

"Be safe, all of you," she said, looking at me, and then turned, helping the children on the helicopter.

I watched, squinting against the sun, which had peeked out from behind a rain cloud. A rainbow arched against the sky, and the second helicopter waited, its doors open.

Russ grunted, pointing at the helicopter, obviously wanting the rest of us to get to safety.

I let out a low growl, which meant, "I'm staying."

"I'm not leaving, either," Garret said, pulling his hood a little lower against the sun.

"Fine," the captain said and then turned, making a motion with his hands. The helicopter blades started to slow, and then we turned toward the edge of the cliff again to bring this battle to a close.

CHAPTER 11
THE AFTERMATH

The Wizard Corps stood at the edge of the cliff with us, a long line of defenders. Their faces set, their wands held ready.

Around us and down the hill were the scattered bodies of the Orchium wolves. They had already taken a half dozen casualties.

For now, the wolves had retreated to the tree line. They watched us, we watched them. It was a standoff of epic proportions.

Garret swooped down and, in a shimmer, transformed into his human form. "There is a train coming from the north. The abandoned lines pass by here, about a mile away."

Townsend's eyes flicked to Garret, not understanding. "A train? Is that something to be worried about?"

"Yes, you should be worried. It's filled with demons," Garret said, his voice dry.

Townsend didn't hesitate. "Fire!" he shouted, thrusting his wand skyward.

A torrent of fire erupted along the entire line, illuminating the night in a blinding blaze. Fiery bolts and searing orbs shot down the hillside, streaking through the air like meteors.

The gathered wolves hesitated for a split second, their eyes wide with fear, before turning to flee. But they were too late—the magic struck their ranks with a force that shook the ground. Flames licked at their fur, igniting the air with a fierce crackling sound.

The impact sent a shockwave through my chest, a deep, resonant thud that I felt in my bones.

Howls of pain and fear pierced the night, mingled with frantic yips as the

wolves scattered, retreating in a chaotic rush toward the safety of the trees.

The firelight danced on their retreating forms, casting long shadows that flickered and wavered as they disappeared into the dark.

As the last of the wolves vanished into the tree line, a smile tugged at my lips. Among the fleeing shapes, I caught a glimpse of silver—my brother. The sight of him slinking back into the shadows filled me with a deep, unexpected satisfaction

Townsend lowered his wand. "Good work. Let's set up a lookout, and we'll remain here for a while. If you don't mind, Russ, we'll use this as a base."

Russ grunted his approval and then crossed his arms, looking off into the distance, his brothers at his side. Together, they made a formidable group, and I was glad he was with us.

Then, he shifted, and his brothers followed. Russ's face was lined, with black circles around his eyes. His eyes flicked around the top of the hill. "I never thought I would take a stand up here on Sasquatch Hill. It's an ancient site. I don't mind if you use it as a base, but please have respect."

"Of course," Townsend said, bowing his head a little. "You'll never know we were here."

The sun was hovering on the edge of the horizon, and the Wizard Corps soldiers pulled out bags from the helicopter, opening up army rations, which they were happy to share.

Morris gathered more wood, and then we all sat down by the fire. My hands wrapped around a borrowed mug, I sipped the black tea, rolling my neck. And then I remembered the cell phone worked, and I took it out, made a call to Maggie, and caught up with her as the darkness fell.

Easton chatted on the phone to his wife and kids, cutting the call short so as not to waste his battery. "Not to worry," one of the soldiers said, passing both of us power banks. "Power up!"

With a laugh, I plugged my phone in, watching the little green bar blink as Garret landed again nearby. "Any good news?" I asked, watching him closely.

"Yeah, I found some dinner," he said, looking at the discarded remains of our MREs with a slight smile. "And, the train stopped, picked up what's left of the Orchium wolves, and continued. It looks like they left the area."

"Good," Townsend said as Easton pulled out his map and scanned it. "Where could they be heading?"

"It seems like the quickest way to follow them would be to follow the abandoned train line," Easton said, squinting at his map in the fading light.

"I did that for as long as I could," Garret said. "It seems to just go on and on. About twenty miles to the south, there is an old train tunnel into the mountain. But as far as I can tell, it doesn't come out."

Easton glanced up at him and then back at the map. "Could you show me here where you think it is?"

"Yeah, right here," he said, moving so that he could point over Easton's shoulder.

"You know, with a little help…"

"My orders don't include a full frontal assault on a potential hell gate." Townsend pursed his lips. "We don't know what we are going into. It's too dangerous without more information."

"Sir!" one of the guards said. This guard was crouching at the edge, a pair of binoculars held loosely in his hand. "A lone wolf is approaching."

I shifted almost immediately, my teacup spilling to the ground. I scrambled to the edge and lowered myself flat to the ground.

My eyes could make out the lone wolf running up the hill, and my nose smelled him on the updraft. I looked back at Easton and gave him a yip.

"I think she wants me to come with her," Easton said, standing up with his wand in his hand.

I nodded and began to head down the steep trail. Easton followed me, probably wondering what I was up to. The other wizards stood at the edge of the cliff, watching us closely.

The wolf approaching us was female, with a limp. She wasn't Orchium or Lowell. That meant she must be an Aldeen wolf.

She approached me with her head down submissively. She gave a low whine, and I realized she wanted help.

I approached her slowly, keeping my eyes on hers, waiting to see if this was all a ruse. But I didn't see animosity there, I saw only pain.

She let me get remarkably close. I touched her with my nose, a friendly gesture. She again lowered her head and whimpered. I turned slowly, showing her my back, and began to walk back up the hill. This was a sign to her that she was welcome and that she should follow me back to my nest.

She followed me, limping along slowly. Easton, obviously confused, followed, his wand still held loose in his hand. She looked at him once or twice, but when he made no move to attack her, she continued to follow me.

Once we reached the top, I paused, shifting slowly. "The wolf here is not a foe," I said, waiting.

She slowly arrived, and when she saw I had shifted, she joined me.

She was tall, with long blonde hair and eyes that looked haunted. She was obviously heavily pregnant, and I recognized her as the wolf we had met before when the Aldeen's chased us out of their territory.

She wore a pair of jeans that were shredded, and her pant leg was crusty with dried red blood. "My name is Lettie Aldeen, and my pack has been attacked," she said, stumbling on her feet.

Easton moved closer to her, offering her his hand for support. "I can help you," he said, leading her over to a rock to sit on.

"I'm Sam Silverthorn, leader of the Silverthorn Pack from West Virginia. Who attacked you?" I said, already knowing the answer.

"Orchium," she whispered, her voice trembling as her eyes filled with pain. "They took our territory, killed our leader...and my mate." Her voice broke, and her face crumpled, the weight of her loss overwhelming her. Tears spilled down her cheeks, her shoulders shaking as she began to cry.

Easton knelt beside her, his expression softening with sympathy. He spoke to her gently, his voice a low murmur meant to soothe. As he did, he carefully rolled up her pant leg, revealing the wound.

She winced, clenching her fists in her lap. The bite marks were raw and angry, evidence of the brutal attack she'd endured. It was a miracle she had made it out alive.

I glanced at Townsend. "We have to put a stop to Orchium and this evil plan. Lettie, I think you should come back with us, to the Wright Lodge. You can get prenatal care, and we can make sure your baby is okay."

She nodded, still looking at the ground. Her arms went around herself, and I approached her, putting my arm around her gently. "I promise we are going to put a stop to Orchium and my brother if it's the last thing I do."

She nodded, her eyes still filled with tears, as Easton healed her with his magic, healing the damage to her leg in one swoop of his magic-filled hand.

CHAPTER 12
BACK TO CIVILIZATION

stayed close to Lettie during the night, and we quickly bonded. She was pale and delicate, like a wilted flower. In the morning, we gathered our things and prepared to leave.

I suspect her loss was just hitting her, and she looked out the helicopter's window mournfully as the vehicle rose in the air, her hand on her stomach. Blake had given her a quick look this morning and said her baby still appeared healthy.

Lettie wanted to howl out her grief, I'm sure. She had lost her mate, her pack identity, and her home all because of Orchium.

I squeezed her hand as the helicopter lifted into the air and gave her a quick smile. "You're going to love the Wright Lodge, and you can stay with me if you want a friend."

She nodded, wiping a tear away from her cheek as we settled back in our seats for the trip.

Finally, the Wright Lodge appeared, its tidy lawn an emerald clearing in the trees, the town of Ashford a knot of civilization. The helicopter landed behind fluttering caution tape, put there in anticipation of our arrival.

Russ tumbled out the door first, and then his brothers, and then us. We retreated to the porch of the lodge and watched the helicopter rise back into the sky as the air from the rotors buffeted our faces.

Russ opened the door for us, and we all went inside with a sigh of relief. "That is a way to make an entrance," Pearl Wright said from behind the reception desk. She looked at us over her reading glasses and then took them off. "I think some people are going to be happy you are here!"

And from an adjoining conference room, the six children and Angela emerged. "I'm so glad you are back," she said with a smile. "I've been trying to get the children settled in. Your parents have been wonderful."

Russ's shoulders relaxed, and he put down his bag next to the desk. "We took care of Sasquatch Hill, although I'll have to return at some point and restock it with logs and rocks. We went through a bunch."

One of the Sasquatch boys laughed, nodding with bright eyes. "It was kind of fun, though. But I wish we were home."

Mr. Wright came out of the room, walking a little slower. "Oh, we've had fun with these little ones. It's like having grandkids. I forgot how much fun it is to show the little 'squatches a few things."

"He took them out for a field trip around the resort this morning," Pearl confided, a smile of pride on her face. "We've got Angela and the children all set up in our presidential suite. It wasn't booked, anyway."

I looked over at Lettie, who was practically hiding behind me, her arms around her chest. I put my arm around her gently. "Mrs. Wright, we have another friend who is joining us. This is Lettie, she's a werewolf, like me. She can join me in my room. It's got two beds."

"Of course, dear," she said kindly, looking inquisitively at Lettie and her bulging stomach. I knew she wanted to know her story, but right now was not the time to tell it.

"I'm going to need a conference room for the next few days, Mrs. Wright," Easton said, looking already anxious to get to work. "And we are going to have some army types show up. Can we reserve a block of rooms for them? Potentia Security will foot the charges. Business expense."

She nodded, a smile on her face. I got the impression she was happy to fill rooms. "Of course, of course! It's like a whole dang convention here at the resort lately!"

"It's the oddest convention ever," Russ said, clapping Easton on the back.

The pair let out a huge laugh while Garret strolled in, just landing from his solo flight back from the hill. "What did I miss?" he asked, hearing all the laughter.

"Oh, Garret," I said. "Welcome to the First Annual Cryptid Convention. All werewolves, Sasquatches, and all things undiscovered welcome."

"Well, in that case, maybe I should give Mothy and Buster a call," he said with a grin. "But I'm not sure the Wrights have enough room for an old man with wings and a feisty leprechaun."

"Oh, don't worry. I've got plenty. It's been a slow season," she said, leaning forward and looking at her computer screen.

The next week was spent planning. We took over the conference room. Ironically, we were talking with Potentia Security's Seattle office while a wedding was taking place in the banquet hall next door.

Captain Townsend reported on the activity in the area. The hell gate in the destroyed Sasquatch village had been reopened twice, and both times had been forced shut by the Wizard Corps.

"We are tracking and monitoring these train lines and have discovered it's a complicated system. We have some ideas about taking this all down, which involves destroying the tracks with some well-placed blasting caps," Captain Townsend said, looking over his scattered notes across the table.

"But that doesn't stop Orchium. We need to cripple the organization. Do we have any idea where their headquarters is at?" Easton said, looking at an overhead topographical map of the area, with all major peaks, towns, and roads highlighted.

"No idea," Garret said. "But I think we should look more into that train tunnel that doesn't seem to have an exit."

The table went quiet as we all considered the danger. "Let's think about this. We're going to need to do some scouting before we go charging in," I said. "We already know they have silver bullets. I don't want to die, and I'm sure you don't either."

"I'll send the helicopters to that region," Captain Townsend said thoroughly, tapping his fingers on the table.

The meeting ended, and I headed out, catching Lettie waiting for me in the foyer. I had promised her last night we would go for a walk in the area after the meeting.

"Good morning," I said, giving her a big smile. "Did you get a good night's sleep?" I had slipped out of our shared room while she was still sleeping.

She rubbed her belly, looking sad. "Baby kept me awake."

"I hear that doesn't get any better," I said lightly, picking up my jacket. "Let's go!"

Pearl Wright looked up from behind the front desk. "Tell Angela the Department of Children Services is going to be here just after lunch. They want to talk to the children. I'm hoping we can get copies of their birth certificates and get them registered for school soon." The Wrights had decided to adopt all six of the children and had started the process. Technically, they were distantly related and probably the closest family the children had.

"Will do," I said, pushing open the door and heading out onto the grounds.

Lettie followed, wrapping a jacket around her shoulders. This week, Pearl had taken her and the children to the nearest thrift store and got them everything they needed. I think it was the first modern clothes any of the children had worn. Their clan had been much more traditional, eschewing modern technology, television, and even phones. It was going to be a big adjustment for the children, but they already seemed to be doing well.

We were quiet as we walked to the back of the lodge and through the green sweeping grasses. In the distance, the ever-present peaks of Mt. Rainier stood, and I was glad we had caught a sunny moment from the rain that seemed to love this region.

"Doctor said the pup is fine," she said, biting her lip. "I wish..."

I let that thought hang as we walked to the nearby trail. It was a one-mile loop that didn't go far. When Maggie and I came here on our honeymoon, we walked more times than I can count. I missed her and wished we could wrap up this trip sooner rather than later.

"You're married?" Lettie asked, breaking my thoughts of home.

"Yeah. My wife Maggie is back in Mt. Storm, keeping an eye on the business."

"This pup was our first," she said, blinking back tears. "We hadn't been married that long. We were looking forward to the future."

"I'm sorry," I said. "Do you know what you're going to do?"

She shook her head, her long hair falling over her face. "I kinda…wanted to go to college. Maybe I can make that happen. I had good grades in school."

"That's a great idea!" I said. "I bet we can help you with that!"

"You can?" she said, hope on her face.

"Yeah, I'll help you out. If you want, you can come to West Virginia and live with my pack." I pictured her living with us, working at the distillery in the summer, and then taking classes during the school year at the nearby community college.

"I don't know…I've lived here my whole life," she said, looking up at the mountain sadly. "I'll think about it. I don't know if I can go live with the Lowell's. We don't really get along that well."

"Why not?" I asked. "Two packs, living fairly close nearby. I thought you would get along better."

"Old territorial nonsense. Years ago, they leased some land from us for lumbering. Then, they completely stripped it of trees. Instead of replanting, like they promised, they left it bare. The land was returned to us, barren and ruined. My grandfather never forgave them."

"So things that happened decades ago. Isn't that how it always works?" I asked, thinking of my family problems that had started so long ago when I was exiled for being gay. "The silver wolf with Orchium is my brother, Junior. He got me into this whole mess."

Her eyes went wide. "What is your brother doing in Washington?"

"I exiled him," I said with a sigh. "And he fell into the wrong crowd. I feel bad, but he was causing problems. Pack nonsense."

She bit her lip, and then tears started to fall. "I miss them. What am I going to do?"

I put my arm around her, feeling motherly and protective. "Don't worry, you're not alone."

She gave me a flattering smile, and then we continued to walk. I thought she would fit right into the Silverthorn Pack and was excited to bring her and her pup home.

CHAPTER 13
SCOUT

When we went back to Sasquatch Hill, we had left the Wright brothers behind with the other survivors to regroup and recover, but I was feeling unsettled. The wheels were in motion, and men and supplies were headed our way. But in the meantime, I wanted to know more about what we were up against.

Easton and I were determined to find out where Orchium was hiding and the extent of their rail network. We had identified several locations, caves, and train tracks that dotted the area as points of interest.

After several days of watching and waiting, we saw the trains running at top speed through the forests. More like ghost trains, billowing black clouds of smoke with shifting figures inside.

Through our hard work, we had determined that this tunnel below us was where all the trains originated from.

But I wanted a closer look. Creeping forward on the slope, I felt the stones scrape my soft underbelly. Behind me, one of the military helicopters waited, its rotors silent.

Easton was at my side, crawling along the ground with me. Behind him were a half dozen Wizard Corps, all with smudged camouflage on their faces and holding wands in their hands.

Technically, this was supposed to be a reconnaissance operation. Garret had identified the tunnel, and we were pretty sure this was the main entrance and exit to their primary base.

Easton picked up a pair of binoculars and pressed them to his face. "I see Garret. Here he comes!"

The sharp stones underneath me were very uncomfortable. I whined and narrowed my eyes. I could just make out a black speck flying out of the tunnel.

Garret caught the wind and soared upward to us, flying over the peak of the slope to our hidden position, landing just a few feet away.

He shifted in a blaze of purple, his head lowered. There was not a speck of shade up here to provide comfort for him, and he quickly raised his hood and remained hunched over.

"The cave is empty and quiet, but there are signs of activity. There is an empty train parked just inside. It's probably safe to approach and investigate," he said in his quiet voice.

Easton glanced back at the men. "What do you say, should we poke around?"

Of course, the Wizard Corps responded with a hearty "hell yes." I was a little more unsure. We weren't at full capacity, and to me, knowing where they were located was the prime reason for coming here. I wasn't here to die, but leave it to a group of wizards to be gun-ho.

Easton must have caught the hesitation in my eyes. "We won't go far in. I just want to get a look at that train."

If I could have shrugged, I would have. Instead, I lifted my nose and sniffed the air. There were no wolf smells, but that wasn't a surprise. So, I got to my feet, glad to be off the rocks. Taking a few steps forward, I looked behind me impatiently.

"I guess Sam wants to go. Let's move out!" Easton said, with a grin on his face. The Wizard Corps scrambled to their feet, and we began to run down the slope, leaving only the helicopter crew behind.

Approaching the tunnel entrance, I felt a sense of dread. The blackness seemed malevolent and dangerous. I stopped at the entrance, sniffing. Only a faint smell of smoke.

Hesitantly, I stepped into the darkness, taking a moment for my senses to adjust to the dimness.

Easton and his boys followed behind me quietly, making hand signals as they spread out, their wands drawn.

Garret stayed by me in his vampire form. "I don't like this place," he whispered. "It's not right."

I inspected the train in front of us. It was obviously old, an ancient relic from the Old West. We had identified it, and several other trains, as a 4-4-0 American originally constructed by Mason Locomotive Works.

The engines' once-vibrant colors had faded, and patches of rust adorned its exterior like some sort of disease. The air was thick with the musty scent of decay, and the dampness clung to the locomotive's worn frame.

The brass components were now tarnished. The smokestack, standing tall, was a ghostly reminder of the locomotive's former past. The memories of billowing steam and rhythmic chugging seemed to linger in the silent air.

Easton stepped over the slightly bent cowcatcher, his hand trailing over the metal. "She's a beauty, isn't she?"

I was more interested in the cabin. I cautiously approached the open door, and a wave of history enveloped me. The cabin stood frozen in time, and a stained and faded driver's hat was discarded in the corner. The inside was filled with tarnished brass levers and broken dials.

The air inside carried the lingering scent of oil and coal and something else…brimstone and sulfur.

There were strange scratches on the floor and deep gouges on the walls.

Adjacent to the driver's cabin, I turned my attention to the coal bin—the fuel that brought this mammoth beast to life. It, too, had a weathered and rusted exterior. It was completely empty, with just the dark residue of burnt coal lining the interior. This coal bin had fueled countless fires that had breathed life into the locomotive, but it strangely didn't look like it had been used recently at all. Coal dust was all that was left.

While I investigated the engine compartment, the Wizard Corps swarmed over an attached passenger car. I heard their hushed voices through the open windows of the car, and I jumped from the engine and joined them.

The old western passenger car creaked and groaned as the group of tough army men entered, their boots echoing against the wooden floor. Dim light filtered through the dusty windows, revealing worn-out leather seats and faded floral patterns. The air was thick with the scent of aged wood and memories of a bygone era.

As the soldiers moved cautiously through the narrow aisles, their eyes scanned the interior for any sign of hidden compartments or contraband. The atmosphere was tense, with the occasional sound of a floorboard protesting under our combined weight.

A sense of anticipation filled the air as the soldiers reached the rear of the carriage. Excitement flickered in their eyes as we discovered the interior had been stripped bare, revealing a surprising secret. Instead of the expected rows of seats, the space had been transformed into a clandestine storage area.

We found ourselves surrounded by shelves skillfully integrated into the structure of the carriage. These makeshift compartments concealed a trove of evidence—packages, carefully wrapped and hidden, containing illegal drugs.

We exchanged glances, our initial tension replaced by a shared understanding of the significance of this discovery. The faint aroma of chemicals lingered in the air. The stripped-down passenger car had obviously been used as a drug lab.

With a mixture of determination and excitement, the Wizard Corps started cataloging our findings. The once-silent passenger car now revealed its secrets, and dust motes danced in the air as the extent of the illicit operation was revealed.

I was opening a sealed wooden crate when we were suddenly jolted by an ominous warning echoing through the tunnel. A cracking sound tore through the air, making us instinctively look toward the source. The walls of the tunnel seemed to shudder, and dirt rained down upon the train, creating a disorienting haze.

An uneasy silence followed, broken only by the distant howls that now reached our ears. "Incoming!" Easton shouted as he leaned out of the doorway.

The crate forgotten, I moved up next to Easton. The soldiers exchanged alarmed glances, realizing that the danger was near.

The rumble and falling dirt continued, and the wizards around me gripped their wands. The howling moved closer, and we stood, ready for whatever approached.

From the shadows, a pack of werewolves appeared, their eyes gleaming with an otherworldly light. "Half dozen," Easton said, waving his wand in a circle. A glowing barrier appeared, outlined for only a moment.

A chill ran down my spine as I searched for an escape route. The wizards moved to the windows, pushing over shelves with a crash of falling boxes and equipment.

The narrow confines of the tunnel intensified the feeling of vulnerability as the werewolves closed in, their menacing growls reverberating through the air.

Spots of light blinked as the wizards raised their wands, preparing for a confrontation. Panic rose in me. We weren't ready, and being pinned in a tunnel with unknown foes in the darkness didn't give me a good feeling about the outcome.

My urgent yell cut through the chaos, "Everybody, we need to get out of here now!" I pointed to the back of the passenger car at an open door.

Easton's eyes were flicking back and forth. "Demons incoming," he said, panic reaching his eyes. Maybe we could have taken a half dozen wolves, but a hoard of demons unprepared?

We abandoned the car and sprinted toward the exit. Easton swiftly grabbed a radio off his belt, communicating with the helicopter overhead. "Prepare for immediate extraction! We've got a situation down here!"

We raced through the narrow tunnel, our feet pounding against the earth. Panic fueled our movements as we glimpsed the ominous red glow emanating from the end of the passage, revealing the hell gate's unsettling presence. The air seemed to shimmer with an otherworldly energy, and the ground beneath us quivered.

As we neared the exit, a deafening shriek tore through the air. Glancing over my shoulders, I saw a massive named one materializing in the tunnel, its form twisting the very fabric of reality. Wolves poured out from the hell gate, their eyes ablaze with malevolent intent, and they closed in on us with relentless determination.

Easton stopped for a moment, setting up a wall of fire, and then we pushed forward, fueled by adrenaline and the instinct for self-preservation.

The slope leading to the exit loomed ahead, and the distant whirr of helicopter blades filled the air. We scrambled to the cave entrance, our feet slipping on loose gravel as we raced toward the light.

The wolves closed the gap, their snarls and growls echoing in the confined space as they reached the wall of fire. They jumped and snapped, trying to find a way over it. Behind them, the named one was coming, and he would be able to easily move through the flames.

We reached the exit just in time, emerging into the open air. The helicopter hovered a few feet off the ground, its blades cutting through the tension-filled atmosphere. With a collective sigh of relief, we leaped aboard, and Easton was the last to climb through the open door, casting a terrified look at the entrance.

The helicopter lifted us away as the first werewolves appeared. The named one lingered at the entrance, partially hidden in the shadows. A bone-shattering roar rent the air, so loud we could hear it over the sound of the helicopter blades.

We soared into the sky, leaving the tunnel and the hell gate behind as we exchanged glances. "That was too close," Garret said, looking at his hand, which had scorch marks from the bright sunlight. He didn't even have time to shove his hands into his hoodie pockets.

"You okay, Garret?" I yelled above the noise of the rotors.

He gave me a thumbs up and then took a seat on the floor, leaning against the wall.

Easton, still gripping the radio, leaned over and spoke loudly in my ear, "Sam, did you see the markings on those packages? This goes deeper than just smuggling. It's some kind of supernatural trafficking operation."

I nodded, wiping sweat from my brow. "Yeah, and did you catch a glimpse of that hell gate? Whatever we stumbled upon down there, it's more than we signed up for. We need to regroup and put an end to this."

Easton leaned in, his faint voice over the helicopter's din. "We can't let this slide. The entire train system could be a front for whatever dark forces are at play. We've got to go back with a team, shut this down, and save innocent lives."

My gaze hardened, and my jaw set with determination. "Agreed. We can't let these supernatural threats fester. We've got to take care of this werewolf problem before it gets worse."

Easton put the radio back on his belt. "When we get back, I'll contact HQ and get a specialized team assembled. We'll need experts in both the occult and combat. This is bigger than anything we've faced before."

The helicopter pilot ascended higher as Easton took a seat next to Garret. "And those werewolves—we can't underestimate the supernatural element. Make sure the team is briefed on what we're dealing with. We need a plan."

I nodded. "Absolutely. We'll need silver ammunition and demon-repelling holy water. We are going to need more resources from Potentia Security. We can't afford any surprises when we go back in there."

The helicopter soared through the sky, carrying the team back to the safety of Wright Lodge. In the midst of the chaos, I took a seat next to Easton and placed my hands on my knees. My head lowered, and I thought about everything we would need to take on the enemy.

I couldn't fail. If Orchium won, this abhorrent collaboration between demon and werewolf would taint my people.

It would corrupt all I loved dearly. It had already taken Junior and resulted in the death of my brother and mother. And the entire Aldeen pack had been wiped out, and the Sasquatch village as well.

It was going to end here; I would make sure of it.

CHAPTER 14
GATHERING

The Wright Lodge became our base of operations, with the conference room as our hub. The regular guests had no idea what was happening. Still, they might have noticed the children waiting for the school bus in front of the lodge, the half-dozen military vehicles in the parking lot, or the helicopter stationed in the back, with the area now roped off.

Reinforcements were arriving from all over the country. Beth Potentia had even arrived with her entire team to oversee the operation. They were currently in the conference room, with Captain Townsend of the Wizard Corps attending a top-secret meeting. We had all been kicked out, with a promise to gather later.

The only one missing was Maggie, and I longed to see her. This operation was stretching out a lot longer than I intended. I was pacing the hallway as I talked on my cell phone to my wife. "It's a bit of a mad house here, but we are planning a big offensive soon. And once it's done and the problem resolved, I'll be back home."

"That's good. We've got the big whiskey fest coming up in

Kentucky. I've got Frankie helping me out, and your sister Katie even stopped by this weekend," Maggie said, sounding frazzled. I pictured her in our office, with papers, payroll, and marketing samples spread out around her.

Just then, I spotted Lettie sitting in the lounge. On her lap was a ball of yarn and the beginnings of a blanket. She looked up at me as I passed and smiled. I met her eyes and told Maggie, "I've gotta run. I'm going to check in with Lettie. You know, the werewolf that found us. She's going to have her pup any day now."

"That's great! Send me pictures! I love babies, and to be honest, a werewolf pup sounds even better!" Maggie gushed over the phone. "I can't wait to meet them."

"Our pack is going to love them," I said, and then I said my goodbyes and sat next to Lettie with a smile.

"Your wife?" she asked shyly as she pulled out a row of stitches she wasn't happy with.

"Yep. Maggie is excited to meet you and to introduce you to the pack. She's holding down the business for me while I'm gone."

"It's good of you to do this. But I must ask, why have you left your pack alone? I've never left this area."

"It's my brother. The silver-haired one. I promised my father…" I bit my lip. "Well, it's complicated. But I need to put things right."

"I understand. Sometimes, the past haunts us," she said, pausing.

"Your blanket is turning out nice," I noted, her even stitches in yellow and white.

"It is, isn't it? I thought I had forgotten how to crochet. My mother taught me when I was little. But it all came back. It was nice that Pearl set me up with the materials."

Just then, the front door opened, and a passel of children came tumbling in, along with Angela and Russ. They had been spending a lot of time together, taking care of the children's needs. I thought they made a perfect couple, but I wasn't sure they had figured that out yet.

But then I saw the way he looked at her and the way he held the door. There was something there, for sure.

The Sasquatch children had adjusted, some better than others. The Wrights were planning on adopting the lot of them, and honestly, it was probably for the best.

"Russ, will you come play stones with us later?" a little boy asked hopefully. I hadn't realized how important these games were to Sasquatch culture. They even had a little course set up in the backyard. It was like upright hoops set about twenty feet apart. The goal of the game was to throw a stone through the hoops from various distances.

"Of course. Now, you all run off with Angela. We've got some chores for you to do before dinner."

There were grumbles all around. No child liked to do chores. She smiled. "I'll try not to work them too hard, but honestly, I think they are going to have fun in the garden!"

"The garden!" a girl said, her face brightening. "Can I help pick some vegetables?"

"Of course, and little Robert can help water, but you all need to stay out of the mud!'

I watched them scamper off with Angela and noticed that she and Russ shared a long glance before she left. "You two seem to be hitting it off," I said coyly as the sound of excited children's voices disappeared out the back door.

"Um, well. Yeah," Russ said, his face slightly flushing. "I'm having fun helping her with the kids."

"I think it might be more than that," I said, teasing him

gently. Honestly, I was happy to see love blooming between the two.

He cleared his throat. "It's fun to teach the kids Sasquatch skills like my parents did with me. You know, there aren't many of us left now."

"How bad is it?" I asked, wondering if the population of Sasquatch in this area would ever recover.

Russ's eyes were shadowed, concern filled his face. "The decimation of Angela's village is catastrophic for us. Morris and Blake flew up there and cleaned up the area. We don't want any evidence of us to remain. Last rites, so to speak."

"What does a proper Sasquatch funeral look like?" I asked, very curious.

"A pyre. They burned down the buildings. All that is left now is scorched earth. In a few years' time, nature will reclaim the land."

"Much like werewolves," I said, thinking of the funerals we had seen in the past few years. I was an orphan, and the loss hung heavy on my soul. Their ashes scattered in the communal fire, just like our ancestors. Fire held a lot of meaning to us. It was life and also death. We gathered around the bonfire, in good times and in bad.

As the conference door creaked open. I glanced at my watch —ten minutes until our all-hands meeting. The Wizard Corps trickled out, their faces drawn and weary.

Easton stumbled into view, his reading glasses dangling from his fingertips as he massaged his temples. Garret collapsed onto the couch, burying his face in the crook of his arm with a groan.

"Long meeting?" I ventured, noting the exhaustion etched into their features.

Beth appeared at the door, catching Pearl's eye at the desk. "Mrs. Wright, could we get some refreshments from the kitchen?

Just some snacks and drinks. We've got another meeting, and we've been at it all day."

"Of course. And I'll get one of Garret's special packs," she said, gazing at Garret with concern.

Without moving his arm off his face, he said, "I appreciate it, Mrs. Wright. I'm famished." I noticed that the scorch mark was still there, although it was fading.

She smiled, and I realized she had warmed up to Garret since our first meeting. This place was really starting to feel like home.

"I'm off to my room for a few minutes to check in with my family," Beth said, bustling by. "Don't forget, meeting in ten."

"I don't know how she does it," Easton groaned. "Sixty and still going strong. She's a workhorse, just like her father was. And mind like a trap."

I laughed, smiling at his assessment of Beth. We had been friends for a long time, and he wasn't wrong. There is no one I would trust more than the head of Potentia Security.

▭

Here I was, again, at the table. Surrounded by people who knew more than me. I listened to the chatter about flame throwers, water, and silver bullets. The benefits of flak jackets and where exactly to set the explosives to destroy the rail line.

"If I don't have a source of water, once my tank is out, it's practically useless. I need to save it," Father Malachi said, and then he turned toward the Wizard Corps. "You guys ever use a water gun filled with holy water?"

There was laughter around the table, and Easton spoke up, "I think Beth brought a case of our standard issue."

Russ Wright, sitting in between his brothers, his fist resting on his chin, had been listening intently. "My brothers and I know this area like the back of our hand. If we get into any trouble, make sure you are with one of us."

Beth surveyed the table. "Of course, Russ. And I've let the park service know we need all three of you for the time being. The park service has always offered us use of their vehicles and provided us with maps. This will make getting to our target area easier. I want to thank the advance team, and especially Garret, for gathering such good information."

Garret gave a thin smile and looked at the map that was projected on the wall. The train tunnel we had scouted was clearly visible, marked with a red X. "Of course, Beth. During the operation, I'll be with the Drakes."

Dallas Drake and his son Beau Drake, the team's resident shapeshifting dragons, had been quiet for most of the presentation. "I'm a little worried about all these trees, Beth. If we blow flames, are we going to start a forest fire?"

Captain Townsend spoke up, "Probably not. We have had a very wet summer. Of course, be careful. We have withdrawn the fire watches at Mt. Rainier and Mt. Baker for the time being, for safety reasons. If you do start a fire, return here to base and report in, we will have fire teams standing by near the northern and eastern edges of the operational zone."

Blake had been drumming his fingers on the table. "And you're sure my parents and the survivors will be safe during all this? I would hate for them to get involved."

Beth spoke with authority, "They are in absolutely no danger this far south. We know Orchium and Junior are operating far to the north. We are too close to civilization here and far from any ghost train line. They should be fine. Of course, Angela, Lettie, and Russ's parents will remain here. I'm confident they can handle any minor problems while we are gone."

"My parents are old," Blake said, concern on his face. "I'm not sure they can handle a swarm of demons."

"If it will make you feel better, I can leave one of my Wizard Corps here," Townsend said. "Just for a little extra protection."

"I would like that," Russ interjected.

"Okay, team. Rest up today because we move out at sunrise tomorrow," Beth said, snapping her laptop shut with an air of finality. "And I need this operation finished. I need to get home to my family."

Same. I thought, looking past her out the window. It was beautiful here, but it wasn't Mt. Storm, West Virginia.

We crouched in the brush near the old, abandoned tracks, the sound of the approaching train growing louder. The ground rumbled beneath me, the vibrations humming through my body.

"Let's go, team!" Easton shouted, stepping out of the brush, his face streaked with green camouflage and wreathed in leaves.

The rest of the Wizard Corps emerged silently from the foliage, and together, we turned to prepare for the fight.

The train wasn't yet visible, but the sound of it grew louder by the second. We had picked this spot because it was right after a tight turn, which would require the train to slow down.

All around us was pure wilderness. There would be no witnesses to this operation.

A few miles away, we spotted the Drakes circling in the updraft around the column of smoke pouring from the train's funnel. Beau, the red dragon, stood out vividly against the green landscape, while Dallas, the black dragon, nearly disappeared into the train's dark smoke. Between them, a tiny black raven flitted, almost lost in their shadows.

In the distance, I saw something appear. It was a gray speck, getting larger and larger. At first, I thought it was an airplane, but soon, it was clear it was Mothman.

He landed with a soft thump in front of Beth, touching his long, black fur-covered fingers to his head in a salute. His large, glowing red eyes swept over us, settling on me. Behind him, his wings spread wide. They were huge, gossamer things with a twenty-foot wingspan.

"Mothy! You made it. I didn't know if you got my message," Beth said, looking delighted the cryptid had shown up if only at the last minute.

He nodded again, unwilling to change into his human form, and then touched my shoulder in greeting. Last year, he and I had gone to England together, to hunt down a leprechaun's coin. It was good to see him again, and I wondered where he had left his girlfriend, Mrs. Evelyn Darcy. A former British werewolf nanny he had fallen madly in love with. The last I heard, they were traveling the country in his RV, seeing the sights and warning people of impending disasters.

"Couldn't miss…the fight…" he said in his strange wheezing voice.

I heard a pop behind me and somehow wasn't surprised to see Buster and his brother Seamus, the two leprechaun brothers. "You all weren't going to go and have an adventure without us, were you?" Buster said, cracking his knuckles. "Seamus and I recalled the last time you got in a fight with Orchium. We made off with a nice little treasure trove of gold and cash. You think any more of that is around?"

"Aye, leave it up to the leprechauns to show up when there

is any hint of gold around," Father Malachi said, sounding slightly miffed as he considered his countrymen.

Beth laughed. "I don't know, Buster, but if there is, you're welcome to it."

Seamus nodded, pushing up the sleeves of his green jacket. "I'm in, then. Split fifty-fifty, brother?"

"Of course," Buster said with a grin, and then he flexed his arms like a bodybuilder. In an instant, the two fae creatures changed from small little people with green jackets, black boots, and the obligatory red hair and beards to their true forms.

Together, their jovial appearances begin to warp and twist. Their skin became rough and gnarled, like the bark of an old tree. Their once bright green eyes darkened in deep, endless pits of blackness. Their stature grew, and now they towered over the rest of the team, their claws outstretched and their fangs alarmingly long.

In the middle of the transformation, Garret had landed, transforming himself with a purple glow. "Just a few minutes now," he said, adjusting his bulletproof vest. I wore one also and hoped it still protected me in my wolf form, although I would have to get shot to test that theory, and that didn't seem very fun.

In the distance, the train appeared, puffing smoke. They seemed unaware of the dragons that flew just above them and the danger that awaited them just around the bend.

Beth was beside me, a pair of binoculars trained on the engine. "It's a named demon driving. And by the looks of it: dark green, lizard-like body, scaley, hard skin, reptilian eyes, and approximately ten feet tall, I would just about guarantee it's Toramongus."

"Always doing the Devil's dirty work, good old Tora," Father Malachi said, hoisting his heavy pressure washing rig to his shoulder. "Good thing you brought a priest," he said with a laugh as he brandished the wand.

Behind him, one of the burly wizards hauled an extra tank with a fast-connect hose. The good father was prepared for anything, dressed in black canvas cargo pants and a plain black T-shirt. He reached into one of his pockets, pulled out a rosary, and wound it around his hand, whispering prayers under his breath.

"Three cars, one engine. We are going to get on the last car and work our way forward, clearing out as we go," Beth repeated our objectives. "Once we get to the tunnel, we will use the train as a base and protection for whatever we find inside."

"Let's go!" Buster said in a deep, unsettling voice, his fist thrust in the air.

We turned and waited as the train bore down upon us.

CHAPTER 15
THE BATTLE

The train had slowed down for the turn, and now it lumbered by. Toramongus's head turned and looked at us as he went by, and he bellowed so loudly I could hear him over the immense loudness of the train.

"It's on like Donkey Kong," I mumbled to myself, a phrase from my childhood coming to my lips.

There were three cars on this train, which was unusual. From our previous observations, they usually only hauled one car. But we were ready. As the train moved by, the team began jumping on. The Wizard Corps grabbed onto the middle car, their hands grasping onto the rail as they swung up onto the stairs that led to the passenger car.

They went quickly, one or two wizards at a time. Beth looked like she was having the time of her life, jumping a train. Seamus and Buster hopped on effortlessly, their claws making a screeching sound against the metal walls.

Garret swooped in, followed by Father Malachi, who needed a helping hand from Easton. He was an old man, and just watching him run with that heavy pack made me cringe.

Then it was my turn. The train was past the curve now and picking up speed. But it wasn't hard for me, I picked up the pace, coming even with the door. Inside was quiet, but I had the feeling it wouldn't be for long. I tensed and sprang.

In one swift motion, I sailed through the door, landing on all fours with my head down. It took a moment to get my bearings. This train car had no seats, only stacks of boxes piled to the ceiling, filling the space.

There were no demons or Orchium in this car. It looked like it was only used for storage. Beth pulled one of the boxes down and opened it.

"Jackpot," she said, holding up a baggie filled with white powder.

"Let me see," Captain Townsend said, taking the bag from her, and looking at it closely. "No way to tell without a lab, but it looks like pure drugs. Cocaine, heroin, fentanyl. It doesn't really matter, does it?"

Beth threw the bag back into the carton, closed it, and then looked up the aisle of the train. "Let's move forward. The next car might not be so empty."

We crept forward, two abreast, with our magic users in the front. It was cramped, and fighting in these tight quarters was going to be a problem.

Garret slid the first door between the cars open and found, to his surprise, someone already there. It was a man with a hard look about him, smoking a cigarette.

The man startled and dropped his cigarette. It flew down, landing on the tracks, its cinders sparking red. "What the—" he said as Garret's hand clamped around his throat, cutting off his words.

The man shimmered amethyst purple as he changed and shifted, but Garret's hand held firm on his neck. Now, a wolf hung in his hand, its back legs attempting to claw into the vampire. "Not a peep, little pup."

I winced as I heard the wolf's neck crack, and Garret threw him over the rail. The body landed with a soft thunk, and I watched as it disappeared as the train chugged forward.

"Let's go," Garret said, moving so that his back was against the door to the next train.

Easton and Captain Townsend moved up, their wands held outright. "Ready," Easton said, his face hard.

Garret turned the handle and pushed the door open. In a smooth movement, he dived into a roll, landing in a crouched position.

I heard a roar and, looking past the other's legs, saw what faced us. It was a half dozen men working at the tables, with two huge named demons standing at the other end, who were making all the noise.

It looked like some kind of lab—probably where they were producing or packaging the drugs. But we didn't have time to gawk. The door at the far end, flanked by two massive demons, flew open. Junior stood in the doorway, more demons looming behind him.

"You shouldn't have come here, Sam. I told you to stay out of it. Now I'm going to have to kill you all," Junior said, anger flushing his cheeks red. His silver hair stood on end, and he shimmered in a haze of purple as he began his transformation into his wolf form.

The wizards at the front waved their wands, and instantly, a barrier was thrown between us.

"We are going to be the only ones doing bodily damage," Beth said, spinning her wand. "Hit it, Father Malachi," she ordered.

Instantly, Father Malachi set his stance, his feet slightly apart, as he lowered the pressure washer wand. I watched as he squeezed the trigger, and a stream of water arched over our heads, landing squarely on the massive demon's right side.

The reaction was immediate. The water slammed into the demon's skin, and it recoiled with a violent hiss. Steam rose from the point of impact, curling into the air as the demon's flesh began to bubble and sizzle.

A sharp, acrid smell hit my nose, like burning metal. The demon staggered, claws digging into the ground as its flesh shriveled. Its guttural howl tore through the night, as though the water was burning straight through its essence.

Father Malachi didn't flinch, his grip steady as the stream of water continued to tear into the demon, leaving it writhing in agony.

Junior opened the door and stepped through, leaving it ajar. I could see him go to the next car, and he pointed at me across the distance and made a slashing motion across his neck.

The first demon let out a roar that shook the car and then blinked out of sight, sent straight back to hell, where he would likely report our attack to Lucifer himself.

But not to be dissuaded, Father Malachi fixed his high-pressure holy water on the other demon. As he burned and smoked, filling the cabin with noxious fires and burning our eyes, the Orchium men all pulled out weapons—small handguns.

The demon began howling and dashed out the door, slamming it shut behind him. Father Malachi let go of the trigger, saving the precious holy water.

Instantly, I dashed to the side, taking cover behind a bookshelf filled with chemicals in white tubs. I howled, not that my friends understood "Danger" in wolf.

But I didn't have to tell my compatriots twice. As the bullets rang out, they collided with the magic barriers, deflecting off walls and ceilings with sharp, metallic pings. Glass shattered as several windows burst, revealing a vertigo-inducing drop-off to our right.

"Shit!" Beth gasped, staggering back as a bullet tore through her arm. Her hand clutched at the wound, blood seeping through her fingers. Pain flashed across her face, and for a split second, her eyes widened with shock. The wizard beside her didn't hesitate—he raised his hand, and light surged from his fingertips. The wound knitted together instantly, though Beth's sleeve remained soaked with blood.

Beth grimaced, her breath catching as she adjusted the earpiece connected to the Drakes. "We're taking heavy fire," she reported, her voice urgent. "The demon's barricaded the door between us and the next car. He's trying to separate them."

She paused, listening intently to the response. Then, with a determined nod, she looked back at us, her expression steely. "The Drakes are going to attack."

We took one step forward and then another, pressing the Orchium men back. They took one shot and then two but stopped once they realized they were trapped between the shields and the barricaded door.

"Give up," Garret yelled, stepping forward. Shots rang out again, but they bounced off the vest he was wearing. He picked up a man and headed for the broken window. With a great heave, he threw the man out, and we watched as he hit the guardrail, and then sailed off the edge, shifting into his werewolf form as he sailed into the void.

"One taken care of. Who wants to be next?" Garret said, dusting his hands off and considering the four men now left.

The Drakes roared outside, and I saw a column of fire fly past the window and a flash of red wings. Then Beau rose with the wolf Garret had thrown out the window. Then, he dropped him again, and the wolf's howls disappeared.

The train car jolted, and I heard a thump on the roof followed by a flash of black wings as Dallas landed.

A scraping sound echoed through the car, accompanied by a deep, menacing growl. The Orchium member in front of us hesitated, his grip on the gun tightening. He didn't drop it immediately, his eyes darting to his comrades as if weighing his options.

Dallas's shadow loomed closer, he finally let the weapon clatter to the floor, raising his hands in reluctant surrender. The others followed suit, their expressions filled with defiance.

Easton and his friends quickly moved in, pulling out handcuffs. I shifted into my human form and stepped forward. The Orchium wolves glared at me, their hatred palpable. "Tell me, where is this train going?" I demanded, my voice hard.

"Our headquarters," one of them spat, refusing to look me in the eye. A sneer curled on his lips. "You think you've won, but you're dead wrong."

I narrowed my eyes, but kept my temper in check. Turning to the next one, I asked, "What's in the next train car?"

He didn't answer immediately, his gaze locked onto mine with a stubborn intensity. Finally, he spoke, his voice dripping with contempt. "Our sleeping bunks," he said, before suddenly lunging at me, teeth bared. The move was swift, desperate—a last-ditch effort to take me down. He came within inches of headbutting me, but Beth was quicker. With a flick of her wand, she froze him in place, his snarl suspended mid-air.

I turned to the final man, his defiance still burning in his eyes. "What's in the engine?" I demanded.

He sneered, refusing to answer. Easton stepped forward without warning, grabbed the man by the collar and slammed him against the wall. "Talk," Easton growled, his voice low and menacing.

The man let out a pained grunt, but his smirk didn't waver. "Toramongus, and a portal device," he spat, the words laced with venom. "We're headed for the hell gate. Once we're through, you're dead."

Easton tightened his grip, his knuckles whitening. "You better pray we don't get there," he hissed.

I glanced back at Beth, urgency creeping into my voice. "We've got to find a way to stop this train before we go through that portal."

CHAPTER 16
BEYOND

There was a screeching sound, claws on steel, and the train shuddered.

Out of the glass in the door separating the cars, I saw a flash of black and red wings, and then there was a tearing sound.

"The Drakes are tearing the roof off the next car," Beth said, flicking her wand. Instantly, the man was thrown backward, right into the middle of the Wizard Corps.

They pounced, and in seconds, the man was restrained, tied to a table. "You've already lost." He smirked as the train gave another shudder.

"We don't have time for this. We need to reach the engine before we get to the tunnel," Garret said. "Let's go."

So we opened the door and looked out at the next car. The Drakes flew just above the train, side by side. One red dragon and one black dragon. The red dragon, Beau, turned his head and looked at us, and then flapped his wings harder, pulling ahead to fly even with the engine.

The bunk car was in ruins; the roof was partially torn off,

and it was smoking. It appeared like the Drakes had breathed fire into the cabin.

Easton lifted a booted foot and kicked the door in. It smashed open, revealing a charred interior.

"Come out, come out wherever you are," Easton shouted, lowering his wand and blasting a bolt of light into the interior.

We advanced rapidly, filling the car with pure force. Bunks lined each side of the car, leaving little space for us. But the Drakes attack had worked, because several wolf bodies hung out of the bunks, burned beyond recognition.

I counted six wolves, but no sign of Junior. These were dark-furred wolves, obviously Orchium.

And then, from the last bunk, there came a familiar voice. "You've killed my friends. I needed them." Junior emerged, pushing back the charred bunk curtain and clamoring out in his human form.

I snarled, showing my teeth, and then I shifted, holding my hand up. "Stop, Junior. Enough. Let us pass. I don't want to have to kill you."

"I can't do that," he said with a frown. He turned to Garret and began firing.

Garret tried to dive out of the way, but the bullets hit him square in the chest. Little did my brother know that under his hoodie, he also wore a bulletproof vest.

The bullets made a thudding sound as they hit him, and Garret lost his balance, falling straight backward, a surprised look on his face.

"Never liked that vampire," Junior said and then turned the gun on me.

I raised my hands. "I'm wearing a vest."

Junior just looked at me. "I could get a headshot in."

Instantly, a magical barrier surrounded me, and I saw Beth beside me, her hand raised.

"Come on, Junior. John wouldn't want this," Beth said, referring to my long-dead father.

"That's right. Our family has already suffered enough loss. Dad, Randy, Dennis, Mom. Throw the gun down, Junior," I pleaded.

"It should have been me," Junior said, a sad look coming over his face. "If you had never come back, I would be the leader of the Silverthorns."

"But you aren't. You didn't have to do this, Junior," I said, taking a step forward.

"YOU EXILED ME!" Junior screamed, pulling the trigger. The bullet hit the shield, ricocheting into the wood of the wall.

By now, Garret had stood back up. He looked down at his hoodie, which now had a bullet hole in it. His eyes caught mine, and he lifted the hoodie to show me the silver bullet had hit his vest. "This was my favorite hoodie," he said in a sad voice and then flexed his fists, a look of pure hatred thrown toward my brother.

I needed to distract Junior. "I was exiled, and I didn't go and join an international drug cartel and make deals with the Devil," I said. "I got my CDL and got my life together. I came back. You might have been able to come back after a while. But no, you had to go and take drastic measures."

"I never wanted it to come to this," Junior said, his eyes flicking from one team member to another. "Why couldn't you just leave me alone?"

Outside, I heard the screeching of dragons again, and Beth's voice rose as she held a finger to her earpiece. "We are approaching the tunnel. We need to move and stop this train NOW."

Junior gave a little chuckle. "You're dead, and you don't even know it. This train is headed for hell. You don't have time to stop it."

"Your master is going to be cross with you," I pointed out, knowing that Lucifer would be livid, we were ruining his plans.

"I've got a portal device. We just need to get close to close it," Beth said, patting her pocket, where a large lump resided.

Junior smirked again, and then, in a move, no one saw coming put the gun under his chin. "Tell the pack I'm sorry," he said and pulled the trigger.

The silence that followed the gunfire was broken only by the clickily clack of the wheels.

"Junior," I said, slumping against Garret. His arm went around me, and I buried my head in his hard shoulder. Grief washed over me, and he cradled me gently. "Why? WHY?"

Beth touched my shoulder. "I'm sorry, but we've got to go."

They moved forward, bustling around me, standing stock still, looking at my brother's earthly remains. Garret's arm was still around me, and as I pulled away, I saw concern on his face.

They were right; we had to move, but as I passed his body, I knelt down and brushed back his silver hair. "I'm sorry it ended like this, Junior. I'll take you home to West Virginia. I promise."

As I stepped past him, I felt empty. My part in this was over and done, and I just needed to stop this train and go home. Beth and her team might have more they wanted to accomplish, but I wasn't sure they still needed me.

Looking over the bodies scattered through this car, I wasn't sure there was much of Orchium left. And we had most of their drugs and their mobile lab. A few well-placed bombs would take out the abandoned rail line.

All that was left to do was to close this portal.

I was the last person to step into the engine. Toramongus stood in the tight compartment, his shoulders hunched over as he leaned out the window, looking into the distance. He was dark green, his skin scaly and hard. His hands, looking much like iguana's paws, grabbed a valve and turned it.

The train jolted forward and went faster. He reached up, tapped on a gauge, the needle wiggled, and inched forward. A fire blazed out of the boiler, and he grunted and then concentrated on the open door. The fire seemed to glow brighter, and then he reached up and pulled a handle.

A long, sad horn sounded, echoing over the rocky mountain valley the train hurtled through. The sound of the wheels clacking grew louder and more urgent.

"Go away," he grunted. "Don't make me get up."

Outside the window, the Drakes flew just off to the right. They veered off, and I saw them begin to circle around.

"We are almost there!" Toramongus said, turning his head. His small yellow eyes looked gleeful.

"I don't have time for this. Stop the train!" Beth said firmly, and Toramongus ignored her.

Father Malachi stepped forward, and I saw that his tank was almost empty. He pulled the trigger, and a wet stream of holy water arched over us, hitting Toramongus on the back of the head.

"Ouch!" He scrambled, holding the back of his head as it began to smoke. He shook it, water droplets spreading out like a dog.

But oddly, he didn't fight back. He turned the valve again as the cabin began to fill with a cloud of choking smoke. "It's too late. No turning back," he said, with a grin, and blinked out of existence, back into hell where he belonged.

Beth rushed forward, and suddenly, we lost our light. "We've gone into the tunnel!" she said, her voice filled with urgency.

Captain Townsend joined her. "I studied this," he said, turning a valve to the left and then flipping a lever close. The red glow of the fire disappeared, leaving us nearly in blackness.

Easton held up his wand, illuminating the cabin with the soft glow of magical light, then he flipped open the left-hand window and stuck his head out. The only thing I could see from my vantage point, behind all the action on the platform between the cars, was the rushing gray rock walls lit up by the wand.

"Team, we have a problem. Hell gate, incoming!" Easton said, pointing in front of us.

I could just make out a red glow, and it grew brighter and brighter. The train was slowing, but not fast enough.

Beth's face was lined with worry, and she held up the portal device, craning her neck to look out the window.

But it was too late. The red grew more intense until a sharp snap sounded, and a flash of red light blinded us.

The rock walls disappeared, and now, I could see the red rocky expanse of hell, pools of lava to our right, and a red rocky ridge to our left.

I looked behind me, and I could see the gate behind us, an inky black hole. It shimmered, and a horde of demons flowed over the ridge.

"We are being chased," I said, watching their insectoid bodies run after us.

"We are trapped," Beth said, her voice sounding desperate. She touched the watch on her wrist, a concerned look on her face. "Just a reminder team. One minute in hell is one week outside. The clock's ticking."

CHAPTER 17
SHOWDOWN

"Bring 'em on!" Buster shouted from behind me. He and his brother, both in their fearsome forms, lunged toward the windows of the train.

I felt the train beginning to slow of its own accord. It went around a corner, and I craned my neck out the window, seeing a half dozen trains waiting, with their back cars open and boxes piled high.

All around were insectoid demons, red skin, thin, wiry bodies, loading boxes mindlessly from one car to another. In the middle of it all, standing unmoving, was Lucifer himself, glaring at us across the distance as if he knew trouble when he saw it. He raised his red hand, pointing one clawed hand across the space between him and the train.

Instantly, the demons working dropped their boxes, turned their beady little eyes on us, and swarmed like a hill of red ants.

"It's some sort of depot!" I shouted, pulling my head in. "Demon hordes incoming."

We spread out as much as we could in the cramped space as the train came to a final shuddering stop.

"Our only hope is to hold out as long as we can, maybe clear a path to a portal, and escape," Beth said, her voice desperate as the shrieking horde hit the train car from both sides. It shuddered and swayed, and demons began trying to climb in the windows.

If the windows weren't broken before, they were now, and the shattering of glass from the cars behind us warned us we were surrounded.

As the insectoid faces appeared, snarling and hissing as they tried to reach us, the Wizard Corps began shooting fireballs toward the windows.

"Switch me out." Father Malachi shouted as his power washer gave one final wheeze and sputter of water.

"Save the new tank," Beth yelled as I tried to get out of the way of whizzing fireballs. There wasn't much I could do, as most of the demons who tried to get in were instantly obliviated by a flash of fire.

I growled and crouched down in the corner, watching the action. Any demon that did make it past the wall of fire was stomped to a bloody pulp by the Keegan brothers, who started to sing a good old Irish ballad.

"Throw him down, McCloskey," was their battle cry. "Throw him down, McCloskey. You can lick him if you try!"

In front of me, a demon jumped through the window, giving me an opportunity to contribute to the battle. I launched forward, grabbing him by the neck. It was thin but hard, like a rubber hose. I shook my head, and its neck snapped like a dry twig.

Then, suddenly, the onslaught stopped. We stood panting, waiting as we heard the chattering of the demons just beyond the walls of the train. A voice, heavy and dripping with evil, shook the air. "Come out," it demanded. "I want to speak to you."

"It's a trick. We should know. We are tricksters," Buster said, turning and giving his brother Seamus a fist bump.

"Doesn't seem safe, Beth," Easton said, looking out the window. "But they are pushing back and making a tiny path in a sea of demons."

We waited a moment, and I saw Beth looking out the window with a calculated eye. "Let's make the ole bastard wait."

The minutes were ticking by. We had been here at least ten minutes. Ten weeks. I felt sick. Maggie would be missing me, not to mention the rest of our families.

But I didn't think the Drakes and Mothy had gone through the portal. They would have retreated…

Just then, we heard a blast and saw a column of fire erupt from above.

"It's the Drakes." Beth said, her voice rising in excitement. She fist-bumped the air. "Come through to save the day!"

And then I saw another figure, his red eyes glowing. "And Mothy." I said. Somehow, he looked bigger, and he approached the train. We heard a thump as he landed on the roof. And then his head appeared, upside down, behind the back window. "There is a portal, five hundred feet off the right side. You just need to clear your own path."

"Let's go," Beth said. "Time's a wasting. Mothy, tell the Drakes to burn as many of the trains as possible!"

"I'm on it, boss," he said, giving her a wink, and then he was gone in a rush of hot air.

"Okay, Buster, Seamus, I need you to bust the driver's door open, and then Father Malachi, you and Sam are going to stay in the middle of the wizards as we fight to the portal."

"Got it," Father Malachi said with a grin that could only be described as jovial. "Do our Leprechaun friends know any more songs to give us a wee little inspiration?"

"Of course." Buster said with a grin as he and his brother moved to the door, lifting one massive furry troll foot and smashing it as they began to sing "The Belfast Brigade."

The door flew open, smashing against the outer wall of the cabin. But the demons on the outside had other matters to worry about. The Drakes attacked the rail car. The demons scattered away as first Beau, his red scales flashing in the light from the lava lake behind us, streamed a ribbon of fire at the cars.

Then Dallas, with his black scales, took a shot at Lucifer himself, who lifted a hand and swatted at him. He veered suddenly off course, as if hit by some invisible force, but then righted himself and attacked another train car instead.

"Dallas has had revenge in his heart ever since the Devil held him captive here for years," Beth said with a little tinge of pride in her voice. "But let's go…"

We began moving forward as the Drakes continued to wreak havoc on the line of trains. Now, nearly every car was burning. A thick pungent smoke wafted over to us, black and poisonous. Then, the dragons turned their attention to the hordes of demons. Assisted by Easton and the Wizard Corps, the ranks were quickly depleting. Blinking out of existence.

They would regenerate, of course. A demon couldn't be killed, but it gave us some time and thinned the ranks.

We were nearly there. The portal glowed just off to our right. Who knew where it would dump us in the real world. We could only hope it would be close to home.

"ENOUGH!" Lucifer demanded, and his voice shook me to my core. It thrummed like a force field, and my ears rang. He held up his hand, and the demons blinked out of existence, banished to some faraway circle of hell.

He took what seemed like just a few steps, growing larger and larger with each step, until he stood between us and the gate.

"You did me a favor, you know," Lucifer said, staring at me. "Orchium was getting out of hand."

I longed to talk to him, but I stayed in my wolf form, my eyes narrowing at him. Beth spoke for me. "Why? Why did you do all this? It seems…excessive."

"It seemed like a good idea at the time. But then, Orchium got greedy. I should have expected it. They kept hauling these old engines here, and with a little enchantment, they were running again. It was a brilliant way to move drugs around the world, using hell as a depot."

"But you didn't expect it to get so big, did you?" Beth said, staring at her nemesis with a hard glance.

"No, quite inconvenient to my normal peace," he said, his voice low, his eyes raking over our team.

"Well, we will be going now. Times a ticking," Beth said, inching toward the portal.

The Devil laughed, a deep belly laugh. "No, I don't think so. See, you still have my daughter, Beth. I want Eliana back, and then you can leave." He snapped his fingers, and the portal disappeared in the blink of an eye.

"Absolutely not. She's just a child," Beth said, her eyes flashing. She raised her wand threateningly.

Eliana Potentia. Adopted daughter of Beth and Dan, secret daughter of the Devil himself. Born in ashes, raised in love. She had her own powers, and Beth was fiercely protective of the little girl. There was no way she would turn her over to Daddy dearest.

Rage washed over Lucifer's face, and he reached over and picked up Beth. Her wand dropped to the ground and rolled away. "You will regret THAT."

But the team sprang into action. Father Malachi's power washer hummed to life, ready to go with the spare tank. The stream of high-powered holy water hit him square in the chest, and with a howl, he dropped Beth and swatted at the spot, now smoking. "It burns! It burns."

Easton and his Wizard Corps threw up their magical shields as Beth scrambled to her feet.

The Drakes swooped down. Beau grabbed her in his red talons, and Dallas grabbed Easton in his black talons. Mothy landed in front of us as the Devil danced behind us. He held a portal device in his hands, and he twisted it a few times.

The same portal the Devil had shut sprang back open. "Goooooo fools!" he hissed, pointing to the door.

You didn't have to tell me twice, I sprang across the distance, feeling the hard black rocks under my paws, but Buster and Seamus were already ahead of me, and they slipped through the portal first.

"Escaped again!" the Devil howled, the smoke becoming thicker. I knew any minute, Father Malachi would run out of water, and we would have a pissed-off Lord of the Underworld on our hands.

"Awww, shut it, old scratch!" Father Malachi said, a shine in his eyes. He really did look like he was having the most fun, his feet planted slightly apart, the power washer wand held in both hands like he was Rambo.

"You can run, but there will be consequences! I will burn you; I will choke you. I will DESTROY!" Lucifer howled. I watched as the stream of water died out, and then the entire rig was worthless.

Mothy slipped away, flying right over my head and out of the open portal.

"Time to go, good father!" Captain Townsend said, and the Wizard Corps held the barrier in place as they walked backward to the portal.

"The world will know my ANGER!" Lucifer said lifting his hands, open palmed to the red misty sky above him. The rocks began to shake violently, and I was thrown to the ground, where I rolled to my feet instantly.

Now, the demons were back, and they were coming toward us like a wave.

"Let's roll," Captain Townsend said, disappearing through the portal. One by one, the team slipped through to the real world.

I was the last to leave, and as I stepped back out through the portal, the only thing I heard was the cackling behind me, and the ground in the real world rumbled under my feet.

CHAPTER 18
HELL ON EARTH

stumbled out in the woods somewhere. It looked like Washington, but who knew? Hell portals could dump you out anywhere in the world.

Looking around frantically, I still felt like I was in danger. Eventually, seeing no sign of promised fire and brimstone, my heart rate settled.

One by one, we all transformed into our human forms, Sasquatch, werewolf, Mothman, and Garret, who stood in the shade of a pine for cover from the sun.

It was a spring day, and patches of snow still lingered in the shade. The world spun in a moment of discombobulation. When we had left, it was summer, and now it was spring? How many weeks had passed?

I hugged my arms to my body against the chill, thinking about Junior's last moments. It was all so vivid in my mind, and tears started to flow as the rest of the team regrouped.

Russ approached me in his human form, crouching down beside me. "You okay, Sam?"

I shook my head to clear it. "It just hit me; my brother is

gone. Really gone." Holding my hand up, I snapped my fingers. "Just like that. And I can't bring him home. I promised I would."

He nodded, his face serious under his ranger cap. He put his arm around me in a comforting way. "I'm sorry."

We sat in silence as I cried miserably, watching the Wizard Corps gather in a circle like a football team at halftime.

The team was all gathered now under the pine, casting stolen glances at me. They were worried, which was touching in a way.

I rubbed my hand to my face, wiping away my tears. Later, I could deal with my grief. We still had problems. "Where are we?"

A warm smile crossed Russ's face, and he pulled away. "Just north of Mt. Rainier, not far from Sasquatch Hill. Good thing you brought my brothers and me, eh?"

He pointed to the south, and I could see Mt. Rainier rising in the distance, snow-covered and beautiful. A breeze hit my nose, and it smelled fresh, like new spring grass and dirt.

Captain Townsend was on the other side of the clearing, fiddling with a portal device. The portal behind us snapped shut, the red glow from hell disappearing, leaving only the spring green forest in its place.

"Why did the Drakes take Easton and Beth?" I wondered aloud.

Mothy turned his head, his face lined with tiredness. He wasn't a young thing, Mothy. In his human form, he looked about eighty. Hunched over but still spry, his hair was gray, and his eyes were still sharp. "Beth and Easton had to be extracted as soon as possible for safety reasons. Orders from the top brass in Cheyenne Mountain."

"The president?" I said, wide-eyed.

He nodded silently. "Yeah, she's a hard ass. Not really a fan of me, but..." His eyes got wide. "I've got to go. I've got to warn the people on Mt. Rainier…danger! Stay away from the mountain!"

He instantly changed into Mothman and lifted up into the air. We all watched, in shock, as he headed due south.

"What was that all about?" Captain Townsend asked, his mouth hanging open. He had placed the portal device back in his pocket and was now fiddling with a radio, trying to get a good channel.

"Not good," I said. "I worked with Mothman last year. He has an unexplainable desire to warn people of danger and disasters. If I had to guess, something is going to happen to Mt. Rainier."

Russ and his brothers exchanged worried glances. Morris cleared his throat. "Mt. Rainier is a dormant volcano. Do you think—"

"No! It's not possible," Blake said. "It's been twenty-two hundred years since it last erupted."

Russ bit his lip, looking off toward the south. "We need to get back."

"I'm working on it," Captain Townsend said, still fiddling with his radio. "I can't get a connection."

"Why don't I fly back to the lodge? Then I can contact Beth and let her know we made it back all right," Garret volunteered.

"Good idea," Captain Townsend said. "Meanwhile, we can try to clear high ground and call in a helicopter to pick us up."

You didn't need to tell Garret twice. I honestly thought that the vampire preferred to fly anyway. He shifted in a swirl of black feathers and then launched into the bright sunlight in a flutter of wings. We watched as the black speck rose, disappearing into the afternoon sky.

Russ was shading his hand against the sun, watching Garret disappear. "Sasquatch Hill isn't far."

"Let's head back," I said, anxious for this adventure to be over. This wouldn't be the first time I had disappeared into hell without notice for months at a time, but I hated to cause my wife to worry. I needed to get home to Maggie and my pack sooner rather than later.

"How long were we gone?" Blake said as we gathered together and put our heads together.

"It's spring," I noted. "I don't have one of those fancy watches, though."

"We were gone thirty-six minutes," Captain Townsend said, pushing back his shirt sleeve. "It's May twenty-third. Thirty-six weeks passed in the real world."

"I hate it," I said, tears leaking back out of my eyes. "Maggie is going to assume something happened to me."

"And our family, my parents, Angela, and the children," Russ said, a long look on his face. "Not to mention our employers."

"I'm sure Beth took care of the park service for you. Remember, with the time difference, she's probably already been out a week or so. She's looking for us right now. An all-points bulletin to the security offices around the world."

My throat felt tight. Having gone to hell and back once before, I knew the extent of the secret organization, but it didn't make it feel any better at all.

We started walking through the forest, and to be honest, my mind was elsewhere, worried about things back in Mt. Storm. Was the pack okay? Was Maggie worried sick about me? And poor Lettie here at the lodge. Had she had her werewolf pup yet? Was she still even at the lodge?

I barely noticed when the forest around us went deathly still and quiet. Animals scampered across the path, running from something. I looked up as the squirrel ran inches from my shoe, finally noticing something was wrong. Then, the ground started to shake.

Captain Townsend yelled, "Earthquake!" and covered his head as he dived into a bush.

I quickly followed him into the brush, my hands shaking as they laced together on the back of my head.

Together, we rode out the quaking. All around us, the trees shook, a few weaker ones crashing to the ground. When it stopped, I took a deep breath. "That seemed big. Do you think that's what Mothy was worried about?"

"Maybe," Russ said, his face lined with concern as he stood up and brushed off his work pants. He looked to the south, his concern not abating. "I hope that's all."

We continued through the quiet forest, headed toward Sasquatch Hill. As we began to climb up the path, another quake hit. I could feel the vibrations in the ground before the worst of it hit and shouted to the rest of the group.

On one hand, it was good we were out of the woods. We didn't have to worry about widowmaker dead trees falling on our heads. On the other hand, we now had to worry about rocks and dirt which fell around us.

As the rumbling came to a stop a minute later, I choked and coughed on the dust that had been kicked up around us. "We need to get to the top. It's the safest place," I said, and the rest of the group nodded in agreement, all their faces covered with dust.

We finally reached the top, and it was just as I had last seen it. Blake opened the secret cache and passed out cans of water.

I gladly downed the stale and metallic water out of the can, looking over the budding treetops in the forest. The pines stuck up out of the bare branches, and Mt. Rainier in the distance, just ten miles away.

Unease began to gnaw at the edges of my consciousness. The spring birds had fallen silent, replaced by an eerie stillness that hung heavy around me. I couldn't shake the feeling that something was terribly wrong, and I glanced back at the mountain.

I heard a slow rumble. The others didn't notice it, but my keen senses noticed it right away. My heart skipped a beat, and a thin plume of gray smoke began to rise in a column up to the sky. "Guys," I said, my voice full of warning.

They all paused, their faces turning toward the mountain. "My god. It's coming to life," Blake said, crushing his empty can of water in his hand. "This isn't good."

The plume of gray smoke expanded as I watched, growing ever larger by the second. My senses picked up the smell of gasses, and I felt a rumble in the earth.

Captain Townsend had contacted his base. He held the walkie-talkie to his ear and yelled. "You've got to get us out of here! Mt. Rainier is active."

"Negative, Captain. Helicopters can't fly, and all our resources have been diverted to Paradise and the National Park. We are evacuating the tourists and civilians as we speak."

"What are we supposed to do?" Captain Townsend said. "We are not supplied."

"Sorry, boss. If you make it to the Carbon River Trailhead, we can have a Park Ranger van meet you there. It's about a four-hour hike down a groomed trail. You can't come to Mt. Rainier, though. It's just been declared an exclusion zone."

"Let them try to keep us out," Russ growled, a fierce look coming over his face. I noticed that Blake and Morris clenched their fists and looked off to the south, where the smoke darkened the sky.

"Affirmative. We will leave soon. Have a van meet us in

about four hours," Captain Townsend said with a sigh. "And notify Beth Potentia we have exited hell, with mostly mission objectives met."

"Will do. Over and out," the voice on the other end of the line said.

He threw down the radio, a cross look on his face. At the same time, a massive, thunderous explosion ripped the world out from under our feet.

CHAPTER 19
ASH

In an instant, the tranquil beauty around me was shattered by an unearthly force. The ground beneath me bucked and shifted, knocking me off my feet.

Chunks of rock and fine ash rained down from the heavens, sending shockwaves rippling through the landscape. The air was thick with the acrid smell of sulfur, burning my nostrils and choking my lungs as I gasped for breath.

But it was the sounds that will haunt me forever. The deafening roar of the eruption, like a thousand freight trains hurtling toward me at breakneck speed. The sharp crackle of lightning as it danced across the sky, illuminating the chaos below. And beneath it all, the low, guttural groan of the earth as it shifted and buckled under the strain.

My ears rang as I sat up, my friends all thrown to the ground around me.

"Are you okay, Sam?" Russ asked from nearby.

I nodded and looked toward the mountain. A huge cloud of dark ash now covered the sky. "Mt. Rainier! Lucifer blew it to punish us, just like he promised."

No one argued. Instead, we all looked at the mountain as it pumped poison gas and rock into the air. Fear clawed at my chest as I thought of the Wrights and our friends, who were in the shadow of the mountain. Were they safe? Or were they already fleeing for their lives?

Blake jumped up, panic on his face. "We've got to get to them!" he shouted.

Morris grabbed him to keep him from scrambling down the hill. "Look. It appears the east side of the mountain blew, and the wind is blowing in that direction. Maybe Ashford was spared. Maybe the lodge is fine. Maybe…" His face went white as he considered the dire implications.

"Guys," Russ said to his brothers. "We will get there as soon as possible."

I struggled to my feet, and Captain Townsend gave me a helping hand. I took a step toward the edge of the hill, and my sense of dread deepened until it felt as though I were teetering on the precipice of some unimaginable catastrophe. A fine ash fell gently around us, like rain.

The air was charged with eerie electricity, and the ground beneath my feet trembled again as if it were awakening from a deep slumber. The birds had long since fled, leaving behind an unsettling silence broken only by the distant rumble of the volcano.

As I stood on the edge of the ridge, just ten miles away from the eruption of Mt. Rainier, a sense of foreboding washed over me. The mountain loomed ominously in the distance, its once serene slopes now shrouded in a thick veil of ash and smoke.

I stood there, rooted to the spot, unable to tear my eyes away from the destruction unfolding before me. My throat tightened, and I felt tears stinging my eyes.

Captain Townsend fumbled with the radio, desperately

trying to establish contact with the authorities, while others raced to pack up our belongings, their hands trembling with fear.

With each passing moment, the ashfall intensified, obscuring our vision and choking the air with its acrid scent. I pulled my shirt up over my mouth, a makeshift filter that did little to help.

Despite our best efforts, the radio crackled with static, our pleas for help lost amidst the tumult of the eruption.

As we huddled together, our faces streaked with ash and tears, a sense of helplessness washed over us. In that moment, we were at the mercy of forces beyond our control. All we could do was cling to one another, praying for a miracle amidst the devastation that surrounded us.

The radio crackled to life, its static-filled voice barking out orders. We listened intently, our hearts pounding with hope and dread in equal measure, as the dispatcher on the other end relayed the grim news: it was up to us to extract ourselves. All vehicles and manpower had been diverted to the disaster at hand.

The eruption had created a maelstrom of ash and smoke, rendering the skies too dangerous for any rescue attempt. We were on our own.

With a sinking feeling in the pit of my stomach, I exchanged a glance with the Wrights.

"They're okay," I whispered to myself. "They have to be. Mothy and Garret warned them."

"Everything is going to be fine," Easton said, holding his arm over his mouth. But his eyes betrayed him. They were filled with worry.

Captain Townsend took charge. "We have no choice but to heed the dispatcher's warning: going near the volcano is tantamount to suicide. We have to find a way to get back to the lodge before it's too late."

We prepared to leave cautiously, our senses on high alert for any sign of danger, illuminated by the eerie glow of the smoldering volcano in the distance.

The air was thick with ash, the acrid taste clinging to the back of my throat as I struggled to catch my breath. I took off my T-shirt, the one that read Mt. Storm Centennial, and tore it into strips, passing it out to everyone around me.

Now, I was only wearing a sports bra, but I didn't care. I dampened the rag with water from my bottle and wrapped it around my face.

We may have been battered and bruised, but we were still alive, and if there was breath in our lungs, there was still a chance to save the ones we loved.

CHAPTER 20
THE LODGE

We began to descend Sasquatch Hill. The ash coated everything in its path in a layer of ghostly gray. It clung to our clothes and hair, turning the vibrant greens of the forest into a muted palette of monochrome. The once vibrant wilderness now resembled a scene from some apocalyptic nightmare, as if the very essence of life had been drained from the world around us.

The ash we walked through was hot, and my poor paws felt the heat. Those that could, shifted, and the Wizard Corps marched double time to keep up with us.

We kicked up clouds of ash as we ran, and it covered my already silver coat until I blended into the landscape so well Russ nearly ran into me twice.

He grunted and groaned as he took the lead, his brothers behind us. We ran like that for an hour, the Wizard Corps managing to keep up with us as long as we paused occasionally to let them take a breather.

We reached the river and were dismayed to see it was a swirling disaster.

The waters had been transformed by the violent aftermath of the eruption. The once clear waters now churned with muddy torrents, carrying debris and uprooted trees downstream. The surface of the river was obscured by floating masses of dirt and tangled vegetation, creating a surreal landscape of destruction.

Along the banks, trees lay strewn haphazardly, torn from their roots by the force of the eruption. Some jutted out from the water at odd angles, their gnarled branches reaching out as if in desperation. Others bobbed aimlessly in the current, their leafless limbs tangled together in a mangled mass.

The sound of rushing water filled my ears, mingling with the occasional crackle of branches snapping under the relentless force of the current.

I knew that attempting to cross the river was futile. The murky depths hid unseen dangers, and the swift current could sweep us away in an instant.

Russ pointed to a massive tree, now across the torrent. It didn't look safe, as debris was rapidly building on the upstream side.

"We need to go now if we are going to cross it!" Captain Townsend said, casting a worried glance at the makeshift bridge.

Seeing this seemed to be our only way across, I howled and ran forward. My friends followed me. It was easy for me to balance on the log and run across the treacherous crossing. And the Wizard Corps made it over rather quickly, balancing with their arms out.

Russ stepped onto the tree trunk, his massive Sasquatch feet gripping the slick surface with each careful move. The swollen river churned below as he placed one foot in front of the other, measured and steady. Blake followed, moving a bit slower but just as deliberate. Despite the treacherous crossing, they both reached the other side safely.

When it came time for Morris to cross, the situation had grown even more perilous. The debris had built up so much that the river began to surge over the top of the makeshift bridge, frothy water lapping at the edges. Morris, usually so sure-footed, looked unsteady. His beady eyes were fixed on the tree trunk beneath him, his brow furrowed in concentration. He wobbled once, a tremor running through his stout frame, but he righted himself and took another step forward.

"Hurry, Morris!" Captain Townsend's voice rang out, urgent and sharp, as he pointed upstream. Another massive tree trunk, gnarled and sharp, was hurtling toward the debris pile like a spear, carried by the relentless current.

Morris turned his head, his eyes widening in fear as he saw the danger. The momentary distraction cost him; he wobbled again, more violently this time, his arms flailing as he struggled to maintain his balance. He began to move forward once more, his steps now more hurried and desperate.

He was about three-quarters of the way across when the massive trunk collided with the debris pile, sending shockwaves through the makeshift crossing. There was a deafening crack as the wood splintered and shattered, the bridge beneath Morris's feet shifting precariously.

Morris froze, his body tensing. Then, with a roar, he leaped toward the bank, his arms outstretched, reaching for safety.

Blake lunged forward, his dinner-plate-sized hands stretching out to catch Morris, but they only grasped at empty air. Morris's fingers brushed against Blake's before he slipped into the raging river below. The water swallowed him whole, his form vanishing into the churning, frothy currents.

"No!" Blake's voice tore from his throat, a primal, gut-wrenching sound that echoed across the river. Russ joined him, their roars merging into a chorus of desperation that reverberated through the trees. The very air seemed to vibrate with their sorrow.

They both surged toward the riverbank, their eyes scanning the tumultuous water for any sign of their fallen brother. The river was a swirling mass of whitecaps and debris, the water dark and unforgiving. It was only by sheer chance that I spotted a flash of fur downstream, but it was a heart-stopping sight—Morris was face down, tumbling helplessly in the current.

I howled, my voice cracking as I tried to get their attention. Blake, without hesitation, made a move to leap into the water, his muscles coiled like a spring.

"No! Don't be a fool!" Captain Townsend, along with the rest of the corps and Russ, grabbed hold of Blake, pulling him back with all their strength. Blake fought them, his massive frame straining against their grip, but the Captain's words cut through the chaos. "You jump into that, you're a dead 'Squatch. I'm sorry, but he's as good as gone. If there's any hope, it's that he can make it out farther downstream."

Blake's struggles ceased, but his face was a mask of anguish. Russ and Blake exchanged a look, a silent understanding passing between them. Without another word, they took off along the riverbank, following the rushing water south in a desperate attempt to find Morris.

We stood on the riverbank, helpless, our eyes fixed on the violent currents. Time seemed to stretch on forever, each minute feeling like an eternity as we waited for any sign of Morris or the return of our friends. The river's roar was the only sound, a constant reminder of the peril that had claimed Morris.

An hour later, Russ and Blake returned, their shoulders

slumped, their faces grim and set. There was no need to ask—they didn't have to say a word.

"There was no sign of him," Russ finally said, his voice heavy with a finality that sent a cold shiver through my heart. "We searched everywhere. If he somehow managed to get out farther downstream, he'll go home."

His words hung in the air, a bitter truth we had to accept. The forest seemed to hold its breath, mourning with us. Morris was gone, and the weight of that loss settled deep in our chests.

Finally, without a further word, Russ turned toward the path. Blake followed him, his shoulders slumped. I caught Blake wiping away a tear as we all took one last look at the deadly river.

We had already tarried too long. And the entire time ash continued to pump out of the volcano, with occasional explosions. We had to get back to the lodge as soon as possible. Russ and Blake walked together in grief, and the only thing we could do was walk with them quietly.

▭

Russ and Blake grimly led us through the forest after sunset, leaving a trail through the ash that looked like freshly fallen snow in the light of the full moon. But this wasn't snow. The ash was hot under my paws, my feet swollen and painful. My eyes burned, and my fur was caked with it.

Even my mouth was choked with dust, and every stream we passed was tainted with mud and debris, the water unfit to drink.

A few hours later, Garret came swirling down, his dark feathers almost invisible in the gray dust. I was overjoyed to see him shifting before he even landed.

I watched him shift, a concerned look on his face. "It's bad," was the first thing out of his mouth. "The volcano blew before I got to the lodge. The force nearly knocked me out of the sky."

Russ grunted sadly. His massive shoulders slumped. I watched him shift slowly, his face lined with grief. "Did you find them? Anyone?"

"I flew around the ash and reached the lodge after the worst of it. It was hit by a mudslide and is off its foundations. The ash and mud are up to the second floor. I flew around the house, tried to look into the upper windows, but I didn't see any sign of life. Maybe they all evacuated..." He trailed off, biting his lip. "But I saw the roofs of the cars still in the lot."

Russ slammed his fist into the palm of his hand and nearly crumpled to his feet. Blake touched his shoulder tenderly, shifting into his human form, the brothers hugging in their grief.

"Where's Morris?" Garret asked suddenly as he realized the third Sasquatch brother was missing.

"He didn't make it," I said quietly. "Washed away in the river."

Garret looked over at the brothers. "I'm sorry," he whispered. "I know what it feels to lose someone."

Russ staggered to his feet, wiping his face with the back of his hand. "I have to get there. I have to see for myself."

"Of course," Garret said. "I can fly back and look around. Maybe I can find answers."

We parted ways, and then we watched Garret fly back south. I hoped for the Wright brothers' sake that Garret found the survivors.

We all continued on, and with every mile closer to our destination, the devastation became more and more apparent. The ash was thicker, and now, we spotted dead birds and small animals choked by the thick dust. But we kept on, the lodge our firm destination.

Well into the evening, we reached the road that led into Ashford. A roadblock filled with blue and red blinking lights blocked the way forward.

Quickly shifting into our human forms, we approached the roadblock. The red and blue lights lit up our tired and dirty faces.

"Whoa! We've got survivors here. It's the Wright brothers!" one ranger, standing near the barricaded road, yelled. Soon, we were surrounded by rescue personnel.

"This way, this way!" They led us to a Red Cross tent. I limped along, grateful for the help. My feet were raw and burning. When they handed me a bottle of water, I rinsed the dirt and dust from my mouth and spat it out.

Russ and Blake were frantically trying to get away. "Our parents…has anyone seen them?"

"The lodge is gone. The guests and some children were evacuated. Your parents insisted on staying. I'm sorry, Russ," the ranger said, his face concerned.

"Where are the children?" Russ asked, and his coworker pointed toward a large tent at the end of the makeshift camp.

They wanted us to see medical first, but we brushed them aside and headed straight for the tent. Pushing the flaps aside, we saw that it was lined with cots, with people of every age sitting quietly or gathered in a corner.

"Look! They're back!" one of the Sasquatch children shouted, running up to Russ and giving him a hug.

From a nearby cot, Angela looked up, her eyes red and swollen. "Oh, thank God," she whispered, her voice trembling as if she might break at any moment. "We were so worried." She held the Sasquatch children close, their small hands clinging to her as if she were their last tether to safety. A children's book lay open in her lap, her gaze distant.

Russ looked at them, his face a mask of relief that barely concealed his own grief. "I'm so happy you made it out," he said, his voice cracking. "My parents?"

Angela's expression crumpled, and she bit her lip, trying to hold back tears. "We tried to talk them into coming. They refused. And Lettie… she wouldn't come." She glanced at me, her eyes filled with guilt and sorrow. "They wouldn't let her bring her pup. No animals allowed."

A heavy silence hung in the air as the words sank in. My chest tightened, a sharp pain stabbing through my heart. "Son of a…" I swore under my breath, my voice rough with anger and helplessness.

People turned to look at me, but I barely noticed. "Of course, she wouldn't leave her pup!" I could barely speak, the lump in my throat growing with every word. Werewolf babies remained pups until well into toddlerhood when they could learn to shift into their human form. "We have to go to the lodge," I said, my voice thick with despair.

"Of course. I need to talk some sense into my parents," Russ said, glancing over at Blake, who was talking with a Red Cross volunteer.

"Blake! We have to go!" Russ said, urgency in his voice.

"I'm putting Morris on the missing person list," he said solemnly as a stern volunteer watched him fill out the name.

She looked up. "You won't be allowed to leave this area. The road is closed, and the entire area is to be evacuated."

"Try to keep me away," Russ said bitterly, his eyes narrowing.

"No one is allowed!" she snapped, looking over at one of his fellow rangers, who was lingering nearby.

He turned back to Angela, gently brushing a strand of hair from her face. "Don't worry. I'll be back. I've got to get to my parents." He squeezed her hand, lingering for a moment before letting go.

"Let's take some water with us," I said, glancing at a cooler filled with plastic water bottles. I plunged my hand in, pulled one out, twisted the cap open, and took a gulp of the deliciously cold water. Once it was empty, I tossed the bottle into a nearby trash barrel and grabbed another.

"Good idea. Let's stock up. Blake, grab some of those granola bars," Russ said, pointing to opened boxes nearby.

"Russ! Can we go with you! We want to help!" one of the little Sasquatch kids said, her eyes large. "Besides, it's boring here."

"Absolutely not! You are going to stay here with Angela," he ordered, unzipping his backpack and stuffing in supplies we handed him. His eyes fixed on her worried face. "Don't worry. I'll be back, I promise."

CHAPTER 21
RETURN

It was nearing daylight as we approached the lodge. My wet handkerchief was pressed uncomfortably against my face, but it was helping to keep the dust out of my lungs.

The only way I could tell it was daylight was that the sky glowed red. *He did punish us*, I thought as I examined the hellscape before me.

Here, Ashford had been hit by a massive landslide. It was like hot concrete under my poor aching feet.

Somewhere under this dust and mud was a road. The only way we could tell it was a road was the signs and markers, poking out of the mud.

"Here." Russ stopped in the middle of the path and pointed to the right. "This is the drive for the lodge."

I don't know how he could tell, besides a lifetime of living in this area. The landscape was pretty much devoid now of all landmarks.

But then, I caught sight of a roof poking out of the tree line. "It's still standing, at least!" I said, a smile breaking my face. "Maybe everything is okay!"

We trudged through the path, and as we rounded the corner, we saw only devastation. "It's not okay," Russ said as the full extent of what we were facing became clear to us.

Where the parking lot once stood was covered in the mudslide, with only the top of an RV still visible from where we stood.

The lodge had been pushed off its foundations and was tilted haphazardly, the bottom corner caved in under the onslaught of mud.

The massive building had slid forward alarmingly. The first floor was completely covered in mud, the front door and massive windows inaccessible.

Russ looked right and left for any sign of life. In the dust, nothing moved, not even a small animal. But from the building, I heard the unmistakable sound of a pup crying.

"Lettie's pup!" I said, urgency in my voice. "I hear it! Somewhere inside the building!"

Its whine stirred something in me. Something primal and wolf-like. Getting to that pup was now my only goal.

"Hello!" Blake shouted, headed for the building. "Hello! We're here to help!"

There was no answer, but the calls from the pup grew louder.

Suddenly, I found myself shifting, my wolf body grew frantic to reach the child. I growled and ran full tilt toward the building.

There was a broken window on the second floor. Well, I guess it was now ground level. I felt my muscles bunching, and then I launched through the air and through the window. The frame splintered around me, and the shards of glass left blew inward.

I landed in a guest room and quickly scanned the room.

Whoever was staying here had left quickly; the beds were a mess, and personal items were strewn around the room.

"Sam! Hold up! The building might not be safe!' Russ's voice sounded from outside, but here in the building, I heard the cries of the pup.

The pup was hungry and scared. I howled to let the pup know I was coming.

I got a sharp bark in return, and Russ clambered in the window behind me.

I looked toward the closed door. And he took my hint. "Dang it, Sam. This structure isn't safe," he said, crossing the sloping floor in a few steps. The walls and floor creaked alarmingly under his steps, and he paused as the pup howled again.

Finally, he heard what my keen ears had picked up outside. "It's a pup? Must be Lettie's? Maybe they are trapped inside."

With more effort than I expected, Russ wrenched open the door. The building was out of square, that was for sure. The entire room sagged when the door opened.

Blake came climbing in behind us, bringing a cloud of ash and dust. He pulled the red handkerchief off his face, revealing a clean spot. "No sign of anyone outside."

"There are survivors in here," Russ said as the pup let out a sharp bark.

My ears pricked up. Down the hall. "Coming!" I howled back and took off through the now-open door.

The hallway was in worse shape. Tilted dangerously, with the roof sagging over my head. I heard a crack but kept going, my howls reverberating off the crumbling walls.

"Sam! Hold up! We are coming." Russ reached the landing and looked down into what was once the foyer. The windows had broken out, and the mud had flowed in, covering everything in two feet of dirt.

Blake was right behind him. "The front door is open," he noted.

It was, but the open door didn't reveal the outside. It was a pile of mud flowing into the room. "Do you think they decided to leave?" Blake asked.

I didn't have time for their investigations. My primal instinct told me to get to this pup.

Here, down the hall, in the room Lettie and I had shared. The door was closed, and I lifted a paw, scratching at it.

"Coming," Russ said, hurrying down the hall. He tried the door handle, but it was locked.

"Blake! I need your help! There is a pup inside!" Russ shouted as he began to shift into his Sasquatch form.

Blake noticed and began shifting as he traveled down the hallway, growing taller and wider, his muscles growing, and hair sprouting all over his body.

His thudding footsteps shook what was left of the building, and he joined Russ. Together, they faced the door, and then, with a massive roar, they slammed their shoulders into the wood.

It stood no chance against the Sasquatch. The door went shattering inward, and I jumped around them, hearing more cries of distress.

A pup, who looked to be about three months old, looked up from a nest made in the bed.

I ran to him, licking his face. He stilled and closed his eyes. The pup was breathing heavily, his tongue hanging out dryly.

"Friend?" he yipped.

"Friend," I yipped back in assurance. I stayed in my wolf form, protectively, as I watched Russ and Blake shift back.

"A pup? Where is Lettie?" Blake asked, holding his hand out.

The pup, who I quickly determined was a female, gently licked his hand.

With a deep sigh, I shifted back to my human form to answer. "I don't know. She's got to be nearby. She wouldn't leave her pup."

We all looked out the grimy window. Below would have been the parking lot. Had they all gone outside? I chewed my lip and picked up the pup.

She was already big, about thirty pounds. I stroked her head, and she nuzzled her nose into my armpit.

The building creaked and groaned as the weight of the mud pressed into it. "We should go," Russ said. "What does the pup need?"

"She's already weened," I said, feeling her tremble in my arms. "She just needs meat. Lettie must have been expecting to come back, or she would have come with her."

"Let's get out of this building. It's a loss. We will look around the property, and then we need to head back to Ashford. Maybe I can find a car or something."

We exited the building, all the while carefully carrying the pup with me. She trembled in my arms and looked at the alien landscape outside fearfully.

"Scared," she whimpered.

"It's okay. I've got you, baby," I said, feeling her soft fur under my hands.

I stood near the building while Russ and Blake searched. I heard them calling fruitlessly, their voices horse and urgent.

Finally, they grew quiet, and I heard them grunting and shouting near the barn that served as the maintenance hub for the property that was partially collapsed.

"The shuttle bus is gone, as well as Dad's truck, but Mom's car is here," Blake said from inside.

"Do you see Dad's truck in the parking lot?" Russ asked, his voice desperate.

I tried to remember the truck. Thinking hard, I recalled that it was a white four-door crew cab with the logo of the lodge on the side.

With a sinking heart, I realized that I saw a white rooftop sticking up out of the mud near what would have been a side entrance to the lodge.

"Russ?" I called out loudly, licking my lips. "I think I see the truck."

They both came out of the rubble of the barn, coughing from the dust. They stood, looking at the roof of the truck.

"Oh no," Blake said. "You think they are inside?"

Russ stood silently and then bent down, trying to scoop away the hard mud. He barely made a dent, only throwing handfuls of thick clods of dirt aside.

He knocked on the rooftop. Nothing. Then, he pressed his ear against the metal top and knocked again.

"Nothing," he said solemnly, standing and looking around the property. A black bird fluttered down, landing in the dirt.

It was Garret, of course. He looked over at me, holding the pup, and then at the Sasquatch. "You need to get back to Ashford. You're needed in other places now."

"Of course," Russ said with a sigh. He took one last look around the place, and then together, we left the property.

It was the last time I saw the Wright Lodge. I set my eyes on the future and the little pup in my arms.

CHAPTER 22
ASHFORD

The next few weeks were a blur. The local authorities gave me a hard time about the pup at first, but Russ put his big foot down and pulled some strings, and they let me keep the pup with me as long as "it didn't cause a problem."

I claimed a cot in the big tent and called Maggie. She flew out immediately and held me in her arms while I cried.

Everything came pouring out. The loss of Junior, Morris, and so many others. It was like I was moving through a fog, but I couldn't leave here yet. It was like I had to help these people rebuild their lives before I could restart my own.

They found the Wrights and Lettie under the mud near the truck. Well, Blake and Russ found them. I wasn't there. I had a pup to take care of.

Morris was found ten miles downstream, half buried in the mud. Blake and Russ disappeared one night with Angela and took care of his body in the Sasquatch tradition.

I saw a large blaze to the north and wondered if that was the pyre. Honestly, I wasn't bothered I wasn't invited. Somethings, you needed to keep to your own kin.

We named the pup May, the month in which she became ours. There was no birth certificate for a werewolf pup. In West Virginia, we typically filed a certificate for an at-home birth, which we would do once we returned.

May's mother was gone, and her entire family with it. She was the last of the Aldeen Pack, but soon, she would be a Silverthorn officially.

Slowly, she wormed her way into our hearts. I don't know if it was the hand feeding, but she quickly looked at Maggie and me as her mothers.

Beth flew out also, and spent some time working with the Seattle office, closing up the hell gates. She approached me cautiously one day as I was bagging up food to distribute to the local families who lived farther out and had houses that were still standing.

"Sam. We are destroying the rail lines this week and making sure the portals are all closed. Do you want to join us?"

I paused, a can of soup held in my hand. "Yes," I said, my mind turning. "But I'm not going into hell. It's not fair to Maggie."

"No. I'm sorry about that. I never expected us to go through the portal. I have a family too, you know."

The bag felt heavy in my arms as I picked it up and put it in the distribution area. "Tell me, Beth, what's it like to adopt in your fifties?"

She smiled. "It's the most rewarding thing I've ever done. Of course, I had an older child, so I had practice. Eliana was the gift we never expected. You and Maggie will be great parents."

I laughed. "Never expected parenthood, I'll be honest."

She gave me a knowing smile. "Let's get this job done, and then we can all go home."

In that instant, I knew this was what I had to do to bring closure to this whole chapter in my life. "I'm in."

"Great. The Wrights are coming also, and Easton and Garret have been with the Seattle office all week. They are driving out with the explosives experts tomorrow."

"Explosives?"

"Yeah." She laughed. "We are doing it up right."

We rolled down the interstate in a fleet of unmarked government vehicles. We looked like a posse of white service vans.

I was staring off at the bare, ashen slopes of Mount Rainier. The scientists had said the volcano had been a typical explosive eruption, not nearly as seismic as Mount Saint Helens decades earlier.

But like Mt. Saint Helens, landslides and mudflow had severely impacted the surrounding area. While fifty-seven people had died in the eighties, only fourteen people were dead or missing from the Paradise and Ashford areas.

The earthquakes and advances in technology had given the US Park Rangers and local authorities time to evacuate.

All of the deaths had come from people who refused to leave or locals who lived too far out in the woods to get out before it was too late.

I sighed as the train of vehicles pulled into the trailhead.

The forest rangers had already been at work, closing off the trails and clearing the area.

I heard the sound of helicopters overhead, and a small two-seater helicopter landed in a roped-off corner.

Easton popped out, a wide grin on his face. "We are ready for the demolition teams."

The doors of several vans popped open, and soldiers jumped out, carrying duffel bags filled with explosives.

They ran out into the forest with a destination in mind.

Beth clambered out with Garret in his raven form on her shoulder. He hopped off and flew up into the sky.

Meanwhile, Mothy flew down, flapping his large wings. "There is a portal just to the east here. Spied it glowing while I was scaring away some hikers yesterday," Mothy said, his voice sounding low and guttural.

Beth pulled out a tablet and her portal device, tapping away. Then, she picked up her cell phone. "Seattle. Can you confirm an open portal to the east of me at these coordinates?"

She nodded and then shoved the phone back into her pocket. "Let's wait to get the all clear from the demolition, and then we can close the portal before we blow it all."

After several hours, the demolition team returned, and we headed down the path toward the portal.

We walked in silence. Out here, far from the eruption, everything remained untouched. The trees were lush and green, as if the disaster less than a hundred miles away had never happened.

Only the ashen cone of Mt. Rainier rising in the distance, devoid of any foliage and now deformed, reminded us of the devastation.

We found the railroad tracks and stayed just to the right of them, passing several spots where explosives had been arranged.

We neared the glowing red portal. I felt rising anxiety and physically shrunk away, half expecting an old-fashioned steam train to come barreling down on us.

"Watch out for stray demons," Easton said, his wand held ready. So ready, in fact, that it was glowing.

I heard the power washer on Father Malachi's back kick on as he flipped the switch and pulled the handle off his belt.

Beth approached the portal, her eyes fixed on the glowing gateway to hell.

She was about twenty feet away when Lucifer himself stepped out of the gateway. He appeared in his human form, black perfectly coifed hair, and dark eyes. He dressed like he was going to the office, wearing a black business suit, with a red handkerchief tucked in his pocket. He smiled and held up his hands as if surrendering. "I'm not going to hurt you today. I just want to talk."

She gritted her teeth, and I shifted into my wolf form, my hackles rising as I moved to her side.

Easton instantly cast a shield on us, and I saw the force field shimmer.

"Hold for a minute, Father Malachi," Beth said, her eyes fixed on Lucifer. "What do you want?"

He looked to the volcano in the distance, and a small shit-eating grin crossed his perfect face. "It's too bad about the volcano. Seemed to cause a lot of chaos, didn't it?"

Beth said nothing, but I could tell she was getting hot. "Get out of here, you don't belong here."

"Would be a shame if more natural disasters happened. You know, Washington is home to five active volcanos, and three more of them are due to erupt any time now."

"Are you threatening me?" Beth said, her eyes narrowed. "It's not going to work."

"You don't care about the people of this fair green state?" He laughed, throwing his head back. He was extremely charming and handsome in this form, but I supposed that was the point.

"Of course I do. But I won't make a deal or do anything to stop natural disasters. It could be years before the other volcanos go."

"Well, if you change your mind…" he said, taking a step back toward his portal with his hand held on his chest. "You know where to find me when things get grim up here."

"Wait!" Beth said, licking her lips. "Tell me what you want."

"You know what I want," Lucifer said with intensity, his black eyes narrowing into slits as a fiery rage simmered just beneath the surface. His lips curled into a twisted sneer, revealing teeth that were way too white. "I want my daughter."

Beth laughed. "What makes you think she wants to go with you?"

"Listen, I know she's part human, and she isn't going to want to stay with dear old Dad forever. Give me some time. Let us get to know each other," he said, his voice cloying.

"Time is something we don't have," Beth said. "You'll never get Eliana."

I guessed you would say that," Lucifer said, a cruel smile playing on his lips. With a snap of his fingers, chains materialized, wrapping themselves around Mothy, who hovered just above us. The sight of our friend bound and helpless sent a chill through my body.

The Mothman let out a horrendous shriek, a sound so filled with anguish it tore at our hearts. The ends of the chains appeared in Lucifer's hands, and he yanked them roughly. "Mothman is a demon of hell who unfortunately escaped. He's mine to claim, and I'll take him with me." His eyes glinted maliciously as he added, "Of course, if you want me to release him, Beth, you know the terms."

Mothman shrieked again as Lucifer dragged him backward, his wings beating frantically against the chains. He was inches away from the portal now, his red eyes wide with fear and something else—resignation.

"Hit it!" Beth yelled, her voice cracking with desperation. The stream of holy water from the power washer hummed to life, hitting Lucifer directly on his face.

His countenance shifted, and he roared and then laughed as he took a final step back into the portal. The sound of his laughter echoed in our ears. We were powerless.

Now, Mothy remained, bound by his feet. He was being pulled into the hell gate, his body trembling with the effort to resist.

Russ ran forward, grabbing both of Mothy's hands. Tears streamed down his face as he pleaded, "I've got you, bud. I won't let him take you. We need you here, Mothy. You're family."

Mothy looked at him, his large red eyes glowing redder, filled with a mix of sorrow and determination. "No, let me go," he said softly, his voice filled with resignation and a hint of hope. "The little girl deserves a chance. I can do more good on the other side." He paused, his gaze sweeping over all of us. "Remember me, my friends. Remember the good we've done together."

And then, with a strength that seemed to surprise even him, Mothman himself released his grip on Russ's hands. Time seemed to slow as we watched our friend, our Mothy, disappear into the depths of hell.

The portal closed with a snap, and we were left in a silence so profound it seemed to echo. Russ fell to his knees, his hands still outstretched, grasping at empty air. Beth turned away, her shoulders shaking with silent sobs.

As for me, I stood there, feeling the weight of Mothy's sacrifice settle on my shoulders. Our world felt darker, colder without him. But in that darkness, a small flame of hope flickered—the hope that Mothy's sacrifice would not be in vain. Eliana would have the chance to live freely because of him.

The sorrow on Russ's face as he looked at his empty hands nearly broke my heart.

Beth fell to her knees, her head buried in her hands. We all stood there for a minute in shock.

Finally, she sat up and stared at the hell gate. "There is nothing more I can do now. But he's not lost forever. I'll rescue our friend if it's the last thing I do," Beth said, wiping her eyes.

"I can't believe he took Mothy," Easton said, putting his sunglasses on. I couldn't help but notice Easton was teary-eyed. "What are we going to tell Evelyn?"

Beth sighed. "I'll speak to her myself when we get back. But now, we need to get out of here. We've got tracks to blow."

From the top of Sasquatch Hill, we all held our breath as the countdown continued.

"Three…two…one," Captain Townsend said, lowering his hand.

The explosions went off in a chain, one right after another, rocking the still air.

"It's done," I said, thinking of everything that had happened in the past few weeks.

"Now it's time to go home," Beth said with a sigh. She

turned to Russ and Angela, standing together in their Sasquatch forms. "You good?"

She got a grunt in return, and then the two Sasquatch took off down the hill and disappeared into the forest without even a glance back.

EPILOGUE

Mt. Storm. The place looked smaller somehow. It was the same dirt roads leading down into the holler and the same big white house looking over the little town below.

And the Silverthorn Pack waited for us, gathering around the bonfire. It was crowded tonight, as I had asked for everyone, from the most grizzled elder to the youngest pup, to come tonight.

I held the pup, May, in my arms. Her little tail wagged, and her tongue hung out as the family gathered.

Maggie poked the fire with a stick, balanced on the balls of her feet. It was a hot June night, and the fireflies danced in the still air.

My sister Katie held out her arms, a smile on her face. "Let me see that pup," she said tenderly as she cradled the small furry bundle. "Awww. It's been too long since I've held a pup."

My brother Frankie smiled and ruffled the pup's head. "I was surprised when you said you were bringing home a pup,

Sam. I've never taken you for the motherly type. But she's precious, and you and Maggie will make great parents."

I took Maggie's hand, beaming. "We owe it to her mother. May is the last of her pack, but I wanted to introduce her to you all as we are formally adopting her. We put in her birth certificate earlier this morning at the courthouse."

"What name are you going to use?" Frankie asked, glancing over at the pup.

"Silverthorn, of course. May Aldeen-Silverthorn," I said.

Jonas King, Katie's husband, put his arm around her and glanced over at me. "You've had quite the adventure. And the pack will be feeling the repercussions for decades. You're sure Junior is gone?"

"I'm sure," I said quietly, wishing I could have brought his body back. "And Orchium with him. Beth has said that the abandoned rail lines are destroyed, and throughout the rest of the world, the Security offices are on alert for any phantom lines. The Orchium organization has been crippled and is going to have to return to more conventional means of smuggling."

"I'm the last brother left," Frankie said, staring into the flames. "The pack has been through a lot. But I'm glad it's in your hands."

There were mutters throughout the group, and I stood, looking back at the newly completed houses. Gone were the shacks that filled the clearing, replaced with new construction.

"Here's to many more years." I leaned over and picked up a mason jar, holding it up. The moonshine inside glinted in the firelight. I held liquid gold in my hand. The key to the past and the future.

I lifted the jar to my lips, feeling the burn slide down my throat and curl in my stomach. And then, I passed it to my brother, who took it with a smile and raised it in the air.

"To the future, whatever it may hold," he said, and the group howled in agreement.

I hope you enjoyed the Midlife Mountain Magic and the Midlife Mountain Moonshine series. I've got a lot more ideas, including a spin-off of Garret's story. If you would like to read a free preview of what I have planned next, you can subscribe to my newsletter and get an exclusive sneak peek at the prologue to his story, tentatively titled *Midlife Mountain Blood Moon*. Start the next chapter here.

One day she's the wife of a powerful crime boss, the next she's a magician's assistant riding the rails to adventure.

Carmen Acosta married a mobster. Now, he's using her magic powers to gain the upper hand. She longs for freedom and finally finds it when she helps a mysterious man escape certain death. Now, finding herself alone and broke, she must stay undercover until her husband can be brought to justice.

Luckily, the man she saved is more powerful than he seems. A federal agent, he wants her help to bring her husband down, and he has the perfect plan. They will run away and join the circus, using their magic powers in plain sight to create an exciting big tent magic show. A bonus is now they can ride the circus train, moving from city to city to perform. But things go wrong when the ringmaster shows up unexpectedly dead.

Can they unwind the murder before the circus, and Carmen's first taste of freedom, is shut down for good?

Find out in The Ringmaster Murder, the first book in The Alistar Circus Mysteries. If you like paranormal magic, pet companions, and female sleuths, you'll love Renee Brume's intriguing who done it.